P9-ARB-969

A Cat, a Man, and Two Women

A Cat, a Man, and Two Women

Stories by
Jun'ichiro Tanizaki

Translated by
Paul McCarthy

KODANSHA INTERNATIONAL
Tokyo and New York

Jacket illustration: Yamashiro Ryuichi
Half-title illustrations: Annie Thi

A Cat, a Man, and Two Women was first published in the
magazine Kaizo in 1936 as Neko to Shozo to futari no onna;
"The Little Kingdom" in the magazine Chugai in 1918 as
Chiisana okoku; Part I of "Professor Rado" in Kaizo in 1925 as
Rado sensei; and Part II in Shincho in 1928 as Zoku Rado sensei.

Distributed in the United States by Kodansha International/
USA Ltd., 114 Fifth Avenue, New York, NY 10011. Published
by Kodansha International Ltd., 17-14 Otowa 1-chome, Bun-
kyo-ku, Tokyo 112, and Kodansha International/USA Ltd.
Copyright © 1936, 1918, 1925, 1928 by Chuokoron-sha. English
translation copyright © 1990 by Kodansha International Ltd.
All rights reserved. Printed in Japan.
ISBN 0-87011-755-6 (U.S.)
ISBN 4-7700-1511-9 (Japan)
First edition, 1990

Library of Congress Cataloging-in-Publication Data
Tanizaki, Jun'ichiro, 1886–1965.
    [Neko to Shozo to futari no onna.   English]
    A cat, a man, and two women / by Jun'ichiro Tanizaki;
    translated by Paul McCarthy.
        p.   cm.
    Translation of: Neko to Shozo to futari no onna, and other
    stories
    ISBN 0-87011-755-6 (U.S.) : $18.95
    I. Title.
PL839.A7N413 1990
895.6'344–dc20   90-4967

CONTENTS

Preface

vii

A Cat, a Man, and Two Women

1

The Little Kingdom

101

Professor Rado

137

PREFACE

Tanizaki Jun'ichiro (1886-1965), one of the greatest Japanese writers of this century, is by now widely known in the West, as he has been for well over half a century in Japan. Most, though not all, of his major long works of fiction have been translated into English and other European languages, as have a number of his short stories. If the Tanizaki drama has hardly been touched as yet, a limited number of important and appealing non-fiction writings have already appeared (*In Praise of Shadows*, an essay on aspects of traditional Japanese aesthetics; *Childhood Years*, a book of memoirs).

Among the major works that have only recently begun to attract the attention of Western students of Japanese literature is *Neko to Shozo to futari no onna*, literally, *The Cat, Shozo, and Two Women*, which I have translated here as *A Cat, a Man, and Two Women*. It was written in 1935-36, appearing in the January and July numbers of the literary journal *Kaizo* in the latter year. As Nomura Shogo, in his study of the author's works *Tanizaki Jun'ichiro no sakuhin* (Rokko Publications, 1974), has pointed out, *A Cat* (as I will call it for brevity's sake) is unique among Tanizaki's works in several respects, and this uniqueness is not unconnected with its date of writing. For one thing, it is the only new work of fiction written and published in the six-year period from late 1935 through 1941. Apart from several essays and prefaces, and this work itself, the entire period was devoted to his great translation into modern Japanese of the eleventh-century classic *Genji monogatari* (*The Tale of Genji*). Tanizaki's translation is "great" not only in the sense of being a masterful recreation of the original but also in terms of its size—twenty-six individual volumes in the first edition, and some two thousand pages in the standard Complete Works.

One can understand why the author might have wished to immerse himself entirely in this massive translation project and refrain from writing any major fictional works at all. But why, at the very beginning of this period, did he trouble to write a novel of medium length which, in terms of quality, ranks among his major fictional achievements? Two answers have been suggested, both of which seem highly plausible. One has to do with the novel's particular social setting, and the other with points of contact between the personal situation of the principal character and the author's own recent experiences.

To deal with the latter point first: in the mid-1930s Tanizaki was in the process of ending his second, short-lived marriage to Tomiko in order to wed Matsuko, who remained his wife and a major source of literary inspiration until his death three decades later. Thus, the topic of divorce and remarriage and the subsequent complications must have been very much on his mind; and it was natural for him to make it the theme of a novel. But, though the theme was suggested by his own situation, the individual characters are clearly invented. One may suspect certain links between the author himself and Shozo (a taste for pleasure, multiple involvements with women, and, above all, a passion for cats); but no one who knows the biography would suggest that Tomiko was anything like Shinako, or Matsuko like Fukuko. Nor was there a scheming parent in the wings when Tanizaki divorced: his mother had died almost twenty years before. Thus the novel as a whole is certainly not autobiographical, though its timing may be said to be.

The other point relates to the social world of A *Cat* in contrast to that of *The Tale of Genji*. This classic novel chronicles the lives of the aristocrats of the Heian court, with most attention being paid to their aesthetic sensibilities, romantic longings, and erotic adventures. It is a highly colored and no doubt idealized account of a way of life that was, even in reality, far removed from the everyday life of the ordinary man or woman. Commoners appear only on the margins of the courtiers' lives, as servants in the background, or as figures of fun. The world of *Genji* is, above all, characterized by beauty, refinement, sensibility; and it is one that Tanizaki, who has always been categorized as an "Aestheticist," was able to enter into fully.

But there must have been a side of him that wanted to keep in touch with a humbler, more quotidian reality. Writing at around this time to his wife, Matsuko, he urged: "Your present situation is ideal. You say you have to go out and shop for things like some servant. But think how much better that is for you, and how much more you will learn from it than you would by reading some pointless piece of literature. It is in fact the only way to get to know the real, living world. Why don't you appreciate the chance you now have and take advantage of it?— that's my question to you. I will go further and state that it would be very advantageous indeed to be able to rid oneself of the consciousness of being 'an artist' or 'a literary person,' and actually to live on the same level as a servant for, say, two or three years...." (Quoted in Nomura, pp. 287–88.)

In an essay entitled "A Half-Sleeve Tale" Tanizaki applied the lesson to himself, describing his pleasure in wearing the light, simple dress of the common people in the heat of a Kyoto-Osaka midsummer, and claiming to have found joy and freedom in the realization that he too was "a man of the people." It is as if he wished with one part of himself to reaffirm the life of the average man and to find value and beauty in it, by way of reaction to the *Genji*'s extremes of aristocratic refinement in which he was then immersed.

The world of *A Cat* is certainly ordinary in social terms. Shozo's family keeps a small shop and lives behind it. A trip to see a musical revue in nearby Takarazuka, or a weekend at a hot-spring resort, passes for luxury. Their language, a lively and charming variety of Osaka speech, is, still, undeniably a bit vulgar. We are far from the world not only of the *Genji*'s lords and ladies but even of the wealthy Makioka clan, that upper-middle-class Osaka merchant family which formed the subject of a novel written (though not allowed to be published) during the war years. Yet Tanizaki's tone in describing his plebeian characters—feckless Shozo; his sad, scheming ex-wife Shinako; the willful young hussy Fukuko, who has taken Shinako's place; and Shozo's indulgent but cleverly controlling mother—is never condescending. The comedy is warm and affectionate, apparently the fruit of careful observation of people of this region and class. The comic tone, while never disappearing, modulates into a quiet pathos toward the novel's end with the figure of Shozo crouching in the grass outside Shinako's house and the portrait of the woman herself, cunning and dishonest perhaps, but unquestionably in love with Shozo despite everything, and gradually learning to love her rival as well.

Her rival: not the silly, selfish slattern who has ousted her, but the true heroine of the novel, a cat called Lily. For, as the title indicates, we have here a quadrilateral rather than a triangular love affair. Shozo's real passion is for cats, and Tanizaki (himself a great cat fancier who kept a pair throughout his later years, loving the one but hating the other, Jehovah-like) seems to capture "the essential Cat" in his descriptions of Lily and her ways. Beauty, intelligence, winsomeness—the aging tortoiseshell possesses them all; and Tanizaki's portrait of her is, like the novel as a whole, a convincing blend of humor, sympathy, and affection.

"The Little Kingdom" (*Chiisana okoku*, 1918) is another account of ordinary people, here a provincial schoolteacher and his family who suffer from illness and extreme poverty. The depiction of them is realistic and highly sympathetic (some might say verging on the sentimental—but not, I think, by the standards of the Japanese reading public around 1920). It is unusual among Tanizaki's works in several respects. First, it has no overt erotic component. Its theme of dominance and submission is worked out purely in terms of the shifting power relationship between the teacher and one of his young pupils. Tanizaki never hesitated to delve into erotic masochism, even among young children (as in the still untranslated *Shonen* [Children]); nor was he averse to describing its manifestations in a homosexual relationship (as in *Jotaro*, also untranslated). But here the children are virtually unsexed, and the descriptions of the teacher and the boy Numakura focus on considerations simply of power and status.

Some Japanese critics have hailed "The Little Kingdom" as that rarity in the Tanizaki canon, a piece of socio-political commentary. It is not necessary to believe that the author intended anything so atypical as direct social criticism in order to accept the notion that the period in which it was written, the momentous events that were then occurring (the Russian Revolution and rice riots and other manifestations of political discontent in Japan itself), may have influenced Tanizaki's choice of theme and his decision to depict the contrast between the rich and the poor, the dominant and the dominated, the powerful and the ineffectual, rather than the sort of erotically masochistic relationship he usually preferred. In any event, the type of critic who tends to regret Tanizaki's lack of intellectual or ideological content is delighted to find it here; and it has even been seen as a kind of early warning against the dangers of Stalinism—which would make Tanizaki a very astute prophet indeed, the story having been written in 1918. What will impress most readers, though, is the author's skill in depicting the psychology of the teacher as he sinks into pennilessness, physical illness, and mental collapse; and the shock of the ending, with its painful double twist.

The two parts of "Professor Rado" were published in 1925 and 1928 in two different literary journals, *Kaizo* and *Shincho*. The work describes precisely the kind of erotic relationship left out of "The Little Kingdom"; thus the professor joins the long procession of Tanizaki's masochists—willing, eager, and, indeed, essentially manipulative "victims" of some adored, seemingly dominant female figure. What distinguishes Rado from many of his predecessors and successors is the comic-satiric tone in which his tale is told. He is, in this, similar to the protagonists of *Diary of a Mad Old Man* (where the theme of foot fetishism is similarly highlighted) and of *The Secret History of the Lord of Musashi* (where the motif of the comical speech defect is given even more play than in the present story), and stands in contrast to the darker portrayals of similar characters in *A Portrait of Shunkin*, *The Key*, and other works. For most readers, probably, the professor's somewhat grotesque obsessions with feet and flogging will seem to lend themselves more readily to comic than to straight-faced treatment, though Tanizaki himself seemed as comfortable with the one mode as with the other.

Japanese society is characterized by quite clear-cut divisions between the public persona and the private life; between *tatemae* (what is outwardly expressed) and *honne* (what is actually thought and felt); between appearances and reality. Professor Rado is an arrogant, perversely eccentric academic whose mask of petulant self-importance conceals a number of unsavory secrets, the details of which are only gradually revealed. His nemesis is a relentlessly intrusive newspaper reporter, a man impelled by a mixture of professional zeal, voyeurism, and an understandable desire to avenge himself for the humiliations he has endured at Rado's hands. The "rubbery dialogues" between these two very different types of egotists sharpen the comic thrust of the story, as does the sly narrative tone maintained throughout. The oddness of the professor's obsessions, the reporter's outrageous inquisitiveness, and the distressing physical defects of Rado's doll-like mistress are portrayed with a dry humor that leaves the reader much more amused than appalled.

I would like to thank Professor Howard S. Hibbett of Harvard University, who first directed my attention toward Tanizaki's fiction and then supervised with great erudition and patience my dissertation on the author's early life and works; Professor Anthony H. Chambers, who many years ago urged me to read *A Cat, a Man, and Two Women* and more recently agreed to let me translate a work that he himself was planning to do; Mrs. Tanizaki Matsuko, for her kindness and encouragement over the years; Mr. Stephen Shaw, my editor at Kodansha, who urged, encouraged, kept after, and helped me along the way, as only the best editors would; and Mrs. Moriyasu Machiko, whose initial enthusiasm for "Professor Rado" fired my own, and who checked all three translations against the originals with great care, patience, and skill.

This translation is dedicated to Violet, and to her friends—
Beth Schultz, Carol and Del Shankel, Tsurukawa Hidetoshi,
and Jim McCarthy, all of whom know why.

Paul McCarthy
Tokyo, 1990

N.B. Japanese names (except on the jacket and title page) follow the
Japanese order—family name first.

A CAT, A MAN,
AND
TWO WOMEN

Dear Fukuko,

Please forgive me—I had to borrow Yuki's name for the return address on this letter. But it's not really Yuki, I'm afraid. From what I've said, I'm sure you've already guessed who it is—or rather, you must have known from the moment you opened the envelope. "Oh, it's _her_," you said to yourself—then, getting angry, "How rude! She's got some nerve, using a friend's name so I'd read the letter." But just think for a moment, Fukuko. If I'd used my own name, _he_ would have seen it and intercepted the letter. I'm sure of that. And I wanted to be sure you'd read this. So, you see, there was no other way. But please set your mind at rest—I have no intention of blaming you for what happened, or playing on your sympathy. If I wanted to, a letter ten or twenty times as long as this wouldn't be enough. But that wouldn't serve any purpose now, would it? Ah-ha-ha-ha—no indeed. Why, I've really become quite strong, after all I've been through. I don't spend all my time crying, you know—even though I have plenty of reasons to cry, and to be angry. But I decided not to think about things like that any more— just carry on with my life as cheerfully as I know how. After all, only God knows what will happen to anybody in this life, so it'd be foolish to let yourself hate and envy other people because of their good fortune, wouldn't it?

Of course I know it's rude of me to write to you directly like this—I may not have much education, but I know that much. But I've had Mr. Tsukamoto mention this to him lots of times, and he

3

just won't listen. So the only way left was for me to ask you for help. Put like that, it sounds like I'm going to ask you to do something difficult, but it won't be any trouble to you at all, really. There's just one thing I want from you. And of course by that I don't mean I want you to return _him_ to me. No, it's something much, much more trivial than that. It's Lily I want. From what Mr. Tsukamoto says, _he_ wouldn't mind giving her to me, but you keep saying no.

Oh, Fukuko, could that be true? Are you actually interfering with the granting of my one and only wish? Please consider, Fukuko: I gave you the man who meant more to me than life itself! And not only that—I gave you everything from that happy household we'd built together as a couple. I didn't take so much as a broken teacup away with me. I didn't even get back most of the things I brought with me when I married him! Of course it may be better not to have things around that would bring back sad memories of the past, but don't you think you could at least let me have Lily? I won't make any other unreasonable demands. I've put up with everything—I've been beaten up, knocked down, and trampled on. Considering all I've sacrificed, is it too much to ask for one little cat in return? To you it's just a worthless little animal, but what a consolation it would be to me! . . . I don't want to seem like a crybaby, but without Lily I'm so lonely I can hardly stand it. . . . Why, there's nobody in this whole world who'll have anything to do with me now, except for that cat. I've been completely defeated, and now do you really want to make me suffer even more? Are you _that_ cruel, that you don't feel even a grain of pity for me in my loneliness, my unhappiness?

No, no—you're not that kind of person. I understand that perfectly. It's not you who won't give Lily up, but _him_. Yes, I'm sure of it. He loves her. "I might be able to do without you," he used to say, "but do without Lily? Never!" And he always paid much more attention to her than he did to me at the dinner table, and in bed. So why doesn't he just come right out and say he doesn't want to let her go? Why does he put the blame on you? This is something for you to think about, Fukuko. . . .

Well, he got rid of nasty old me and has started a new life with you, the girl he loves. As long as it was me he was with, he needed Lily. But why should he now? Isn't she just a bother to have around? Or could it be that even now, without her, there'd be something missing? And does that mean that he looks on you, like me, as something a little lower than a cat? Oh but forgive me, I've gone and said more than I meant to! . . . I'm sure he wouldn't be as stupid as that. Still, the fact that he's trying to hide his feelings for Lily and blame everything on you might mean that he's a little worried. . . . Oh dear—silly me, going on as if it was my business. But anyway, do be careful, Fukuko dear. Don't think "Oh, it's just a cat," or you may find yourself losing out to it in the end. I would never give you bad advice—I'm thinking of you, not myself, in all this. Get Lily away from him just as soon as you can. And if he refuses to let her go, won't that seem even more suspicious?. . .

Fukuko stored all this away and began to observe Shozo and Lily's behavior more carefully. She watched Shozo enjoying his saké, with a dish of marinated horse mackerel to go with it. He took a sip, then put the small cup down and said "Lily!" Picking up a fish with his chopsticks, he held it high in the air. Lily had been standing on her hind legs with her forepaws resting on the edge of the oval dining table and staring, motionless, at the fish lying on the plate in front of her master. She looked like a customer propping himself up against a bar somewhere, or like one of the gargoyles gazing down from the spires of Notre Dame. When the piece was lifted from the plate, Lily's nostrils

5

began to quiver and her large, intelligent eyes grew quite round, as if with human amazement, as she gazed up at the longed-for morsel.

But Shozo was not inclined to give in so easily. "Heeere it goes!" he teased, dangling the fish right in front of Lily's nose before suddenly snatching it away and popping it into his own mouth. Then he noisily slurped away at the dressing that covered the mackerel, crunched through the brittle bones, and began the whole process again with the next piece. Bringing it close, then withdrawing it to a distance, raising it, then lowering it, he tantalized the cat. Lifting her paws from the table and bringing them up high on either side of her chest in ghostly fashion, Lily began to pursue the fish, tottering after it on her hind legs. If the prey was brought to a standstill just over her head, the cat would fix it intently with her eyes and then make a leap for it, darting out with her front paws to seize it. She would just fail to get it, fall back, then leap again. It took her five or ten minutes of such frantic activity to secure one mackerel.

Shozo repeated the same thing over and over again. He would give her a fish, then himself a little drink, and calling "Lily" would raise the next prize high. There must originally have been some twelve or thirteen mackerel on Shozo's plate, each about two inches long, of which he himself had actually eaten perhaps three or four. For the rest, he had simply sucked out a bit of the vinegar dressing before giving the flesh to Lily.

"Ohh-ohh ... *owww!* That *hurts!*" Shozo let out a shriek: Lily had leapt onto his shoulders and dug in her claws.

"Get down! Get down from there!"

It was past the middle of September, and the last traces of summer heat were fading away; but Shozo, who, like most fat people, disliked the heat and was prone to sweating, had brought a low table out to the edge of the back veranda, now muddy from a recent flood. He sat on top of it, wearing only linen half-drawers, a short-sleeved undershirt, and a woolen stomach-band. The shoulders Lily had jumped onto were fleshy and round like little hills; and to keep from sliding off she naturally had to use her claws. As they dug through the thin cotton undershirt and bit into Shozo's flesh, he gave another cry of pain.

"Get down from there, you—" he shouted, shrugging his shoulders violently and leaning to one side to encourage her to leap off. But the cat, determined to maintain her perch, just dug her claws in deeper until Shozo's undershirt began to be dappled with spots of blood.

Yet, though he grumbled about her "wildness," he could never bring himself to be really angry with her. Lily seemed to be fully aware of this as she gently rubbed her face against his cheek with little flattering noises and, if she saw that his mouth was full of fish, boldly brought her own right up to her master's. If Shozo interrupted his chewing to poke out a piece of fish with his tongue, Lily would nimbly dart her head forward to seize the morsel. Occasionally she would devour it all at once; at other times, she would lick the remnants from around Shozo's mouth, carefully and complacently. There were even times when cat and master would contend for the same piece, each tugging at one end. Then Shozo would put on an angry act, complete with grunts and cries, frowns, grimaces, and a little spitting. Actually, though, he seemed to be enjoying himself just as much as Lily was.

Resting a bit from these exhausting games, he casually held out his saké cup for a refill. "Hey, what's wrong?" Suddenly anxious, he looked up at his wife, who had been in a sunny mood until just a while ago but was now fixing him with a steady gaze, her hands thrust into her sleeves instead of offering the expected drink.

"There's no more saké?" he ventured, looking with wary surprise into his wife's eyes and slowly withdrawing the cup. She had a calm, unflinching look about her as she announced "There's something I want to talk about," and then settled into a rather gloomy silence.

"What?... What about?..."

"I want you to give that cat to Shinako!"

"But ... why?"

To make a demand like that out of the blue, why, it was outrageous, thought Shozo, blinking furiously for a few moments; but his wife looked in no mood to be trifled with, and he was at a loss what to think or do.

"But why this, all of a sudden?"

"Never mind why—just give her the cat! Call Mr. Tsukamoto over tomorrow and be done with it."

"But what's the point of all this anyway?"

"So, you refuse?"

"Now hold on a minute! How can I agree when you won't even tell me why? Are you angry about something? Something I did?"

Could Fukuko be jealous of Lily? He considered this possibility for a moment but then dismissed it as making no sense. After all, Fukuko herself was basically fond of cats. When Shozo was still living with his former wife, Shinako, he had sometimes mentioned her occasional jealousy of the cat to Fukuko, who had always made rather scornful fun of this sort of silliness. Obviously, then, she had known all about Shozo's fondness for cats before she came to live with him. Moreover, since coming, she too had shown affection for Lily, though not to Shozo's extreme extent. She had never said a word against Lily for barging in on the couple's daily meals together as the cat had just done today. And when, like today, Shozo took time over his evening bottle

8

of saké to play with Lily, Fukuko usually enjoyed watching their circus-like performance and sometimes even tossed the cat a scrap or two herself, or made her jump for one. Thus, Lily's interposed presence had the effect of binding the newly-wed couple more closely, making their suppers together times of laughter and relaxation; certainly she had caused no trouble or bother. But what was the problem, then? Everything had been fine up to yesterday—or, rather, up till just now, until Shozo's fifth or sixth cup. Had some little slip of his upset his wife, to make the situation suddenly change so completely? Or was she starting to feel sorry for Shinako? Was that why she demanded that he hand over his cat to his ex-wife?

It was, of course, true that when Shinako left she had asked for Lily as part of the settlement, and afterward she had dispatched Tsukamoto several times with the same request. But Shozo had decided it was best not even to discuss the matter, and steadily refused to do so. The point of Shinako's message via Tsukamoto was that, though she should really have no regrets about leaving a man heartless enough to drive his own wife from her home and then drag in some other woman to take her place, yet somehow she couldn't forget him. No matter how hard she tried to hate and resent him, it was simply impossible. That's why she wanted something to remember him by. Couldn't she perhaps have Lily as a kind of souvenir? It's true that when they were living together, she had resented all the love that Shozo had shown the cat and had sometimes mistreated her a bit on the sly; but now every single thing from their old house was filled with memories—and Lily especially! Shinako wanted at least to have Lily, in place of the child they'd never had, so she could lavish her affection on her. That would, to some extent, make up for all the sadness and loneliness of her life. . . .

"So you see," Tsukamoto would conclude, "it's just a matter of that cat, Mr. Ishii. You can't help feeling sorry for her, can you, when you hear how she feels and all."

But Shozo's reply was unvarying: "You can't trust a word that woman says."

Shinako specialized in driving hard bargains; and she was crafty—there was no reading her. Whatever she said was to be taken with a large quantity of salt. In this case, for example, her tender words about missing Shozo and loving Lily were very suspicious, coming from such a tough, stubborn character. Love Lily, indeed! Why should she? Probably she just wanted to take her off somewhere and torment her, out of spite. Or maybe the aim was just to get back at Shozo by taking something he valued away from him. No—that was too childish a revenge for her. At any rate, the rather simpleminded Shozo was unable to guess her real intentions, which made him feel all the more uneasy and resentful. Who was she to make all these selfish demands on him, anyway? Of course, he *had* been in a weak position, especially since he wanted to get her out of the house as soon as possible. That's why he'd accepted most of her requests. But he'd be damned if he would let her take Lily now, on top of everything else! And so Shozo continued to evade, with his characteristic variety of roundabout arguments and excuses, even Tsukamoto's most insistent pleadings. Fukuko naturally was in complete agreement with this policy, and indeed took an even harder line than did her husband himself.

"So tell me the *reason!* I haven't a clue what this is all about." Shozo reached out for the saké bottle and helped himself to another cup. Then, giving his thigh a smart slap, he glanced nervously around the room and said, half to himself, "Don't we have any mosquito coils?" It was getting dark, and a small cloud of mosquitoes was advancing toward the veranda from below the wooden fence nearby, with a high-pitched hum. Lily had been curled up beneath the table, with an air of having slightly over-indulged. But when the couple's talk began to turn to her, she slipped down into the garden, insinuated herself beneath the fence, and disappeared, as if out of a feline sense of delicacy. The effect was comical, though in fact Lily always absented her-self for a while after eating a really large meal.

Fukuko went into the kitchen without saying a word and returned with a mosquito coil, which she lit and placed under the dining table. Then, in a gentler tone than before she asked, "You gave all the mackerel to the cat, didn't you? You couldn't have had more than two or three yourself."

"I really don't remember."

"I was counting. There were thirteen fish on that plate. Lily ate ten, so that means you ate three."

"What if I did?"

"You think there's nothing wrong with that? Well, think again. Now, I'm not going to get jealous over some cat. But you insisted I make marinated mackerel because *you* like it, even after I told you I can't stand it myself. Then you hardly touch it, and give it all to that cat!"

This was the burden of Fukuko's complaint. . . .

In the towns along the Osaka–Kobe railway line—Nishi-nomiya, Ashiya, Uozaki, Sumiyoshi—horse mackerel and sar-dines taken from the ocean nearby were brought for sale almost every day, "fresh-caught," as the fishmongers called out on their rounds. The price was from ten to fifteen sen per bucket, which was just enough to feed a family of three or four.

When sales were good, several fishmongers would appear each day. During the summer, the fish were each only about one inch long; and, though they gradually grew in size as autumn approached, in their smaller state they were unsuitable for either frying or broiling with salt. They had to be roasted plain, marinated in a soy and vinegar sauce, and eaten bones and all with some shredded ginger on top. But Fukuko had objected to preparing them this way, since she disliked the soy-vinegar marinade. She liked warm, oily foods; it depressed her to have to eat cold, stringy dishes like horse mackerel. Confronted with this all-too-typical fussiness on Fukuko's part, Shozo told her to make what she liked for herself. *He* wanted mackerel, and he would fix it on his own. When a fish-seller came around, he called him in and bought some.

Now, Fukuko was a cousin of Shozo's; and, given the circumstances under which she became his wife, there was no need for her to worry about pleasing a difficult mother-in-law. So from her second day of married life, she did just as she pleased in everything. All the same, she could hardly stand by and watch her husband trying to wield a kitchen knife, so in the end she made the marinated fish for both of them, though under protest. To make matters worse, they had been dining off mackerel for five or six days running. Then, two or three days ago, it had struck her: Shozo wasn't even eating the food he'd insisted on having, ignoring his wife's complaints; instead, he was giving it all to the cat! The more she thought about it, the clearer it all became: the mackerel were small, with little bones, easily chewed; there was no need to fillet them, and they could be served cold; and one got a lot for one's money—in other words, they were an ideal food to serve to the cat on a daily basis. They weren't Shozo's favorite dish, but that cat's! In this household, the husband, ignoring his wife's preferences, planned the evening menu with his pet alone in mind. Fukuko had been prepared to sacrifice her own tastes for her husband's sake, while in fact it was for the cat that she cooked; she had become a companion to the cat.

"That's not true! I always plan to eat them myself, but that Lily just keeps after me, and I end up tossing them to her one after the other."

"What a liar! You pretend to like them just so you can give them all to Lily. Your cat means more to you than I do!"

"How can you say that?" Shozo spat the words out with a great show of indignation, but Fukuko's final comment had clearly devastated him.

"Am I more important, then?"

"Of course you are! Don't be silly."

"Then show me, instead of just talking about it. Otherwise how can I believe you?"

"All right. Starting tomorrow, I won't buy another mackerel. That should satisfy you."

"Forget about that, and just get rid of Lily! Once that cat is out of the way, everything'll be fine."

She *couldn't* mean it. But he mustn't treat the matter lightly or she might get even more worked up. Shozo wearily rearranged his limbs into the formal sitting posture, with his knees close together, leaned forward, placing his hands politely on his knees, and said in a pitiful, pleading sort of way, "You mean you'd send her off to a place where you know she'd be mistreated? How could you suggest anything so cruel? Please, don't say things like that. . . ."

"There, you see? That cat *is* more important to you. I tell you, if you don't do something about her, I'm leaving!"

"Don't be silly. . . ."

"I'm not going to be put in competition with some animal."

13

Suddenly tears welled up—from anger, perhaps. They seemed to take Fukuko herself by surprise, for she hurriedly turned her back on her flustered husband.

On the morning Shinako's letter arrived under Yukiko's name, Fukuko's first thought was how nasty it was of her to try to make trouble between her and Shozo like this. Did she really think Fukuko was fool enough to be taken in by such an obvious trick? Her plan clearly was to make Fukuko so uneasy about Lily that she'd be glad to give her up. Shinako would then clap her hands and say, "Well, look at that! Jealous of a cat, are you? You used to make jokes about me, but it looks as if you're not too sure how you stand with your husband either!" Or she may have hoped that at least the letter would stir up a little trouble in the family—and that would suit Shinako just fine. But Fukuko would foil those plans: the best thing would be to show the woman just how little effect her message had had by making a happy marriage even happier. And they would make it crystal clear that they both loved Lily equally and would certainly not consider handing her over to Shinako. Yes, that was the thing to do!

Unfortunately, though, the letter had come at a bad time, just when several days of a steady mackerel diet were weighing rather heavily on Fukuko's spirits, tempting her to try, just this once, to teach Shozo a good lesson. She was not really as fond of cats as her husband imagined. Her affections were forced by two considerations: the desire to accommodate Shozo's tastes and to spite Shinako. She had convinced herself, as well as others, that she was a true cat lover, especially during the period when she had not yet established herself in Shozo's household but was plotting with O-rin, her prospective mother-in-law, somehow to get rid of Shinako. Even after becoming Shozo's wife, she had managed to maintain her reputation as a cat fancier by lavishing affection on Lily. Gradually, however, she had begun to find the presence of this small animal in her household hateful.

It was of a Western breed, with soft, silky fur; a pretty female, unusually elegant in form and features. When Fukuko had visited the house as a guest and taken Lily on her lap, she'd thought, "What a lovely cat! And how odd of this Shinako person to find her a nuisance. . . . Maybe when a woman is losing her husband's love, she can't help resenting even the family cat!" This wasn't out of spite—Fukuko really felt that way as she sat stroking the cat. But now that she had succeeded Shinako as mistress of the house, her former rival's attitude did not seem so ridiculous after all. Not, of course, that she was receiving the same kind of treatment Shinako had; no, she was being well looked after by Shozo. Only, his fondness for cats wasn't of the ordinary kind; it was definitely excessive. It might be all very well to like cats, but it was going too far to transfer a fish from master's mouth to cat's, or to pull at either end of it in a kind of tug-of-war (and in front of one's own wife, too).

Even the very fact of Lily being present at their dinner table annoyed Fukuko, to tell the truth. Her mother-in-law was tactful enough to finish her evening meal early and then go up to the second floor, leaving Fukuko to enjoy her husband's company alone; but then that cat would sneak in and grab Shozo's attention away from her. Sometimes in the evening she thought the cat was blessedly absent, but at the sound of the dining table's legs being unfolded, or at the clatter of dishes, Lily would suddenly appear. On those rare occasions when she did not present herself, Shozo, outrageously, would call her in a loud voice: "Liii-ly . . . Liiily. . . ." Up to the second floor, back to the rear entrance, even out into the street in front he would go, calling her

15

name again and again, until she reappeared.

"She'll be back soon—why don't you have a little saké?" Fukuko would say, lifting the warm flask; but he would hesitate, unable to settle down. At such times, all he could think of was Lily: it didn't occur to him to wonder what his wife was thinking.

Then there was the business of Lily coming into their bed at night—Fukuko didn't care much for that either. Shozo had raised three cats in all, but Lily was the only one clever enough to crawl in under the mosquito net, as he proudly said. And indeed it was so: flattening her head against the tatami mat, the cat would slip in under the bottom of the net. Usually she would curl up next to Shozo's mattress; but when it was chilly, she climbed onto the quilt and then worked her way down from the pillow deep into the bedclothes, slipping under them as she had with the mosquito net. Truly, husband and wife could hide no secrets whatsoever from Lily.

Still, Fukuko had managed to keep her real feelings about the cat hidden, partly because there had been no clear opportunity to take off the mask of cat fancier and show her actual dislike, but also because of vanity—her rival, after all, was only a cat. "Lily's just something for him to play with: I'm the one he loves. He'd be lost without me. I mustn't do anything silly, anything that would cheapen myself in his eyes. I've just got to relax and stop blaming that harmless little animal." And so she tried to change her attitude and go along with her husband's wishes; but Fukuko was not by nature a very long-suffering person, and it was hardly to be expected that she would put up with this situation indefinitely. Then, just as her displeasure was slowly beginning to mount again, and to show itself at times in her expression, there was the incident of the marinated mackerel. Her husband, in order to please that cat, insisted on a dish that she personally couldn't stand; and he did this by pretending he was

16

fond of it himself, putting on an act for her benefit. Obviously, when wife and cat were put in the balance, the cat won. She had tried to ignore the fact, but now he was rubbing her nose in it. There was no room for vanity any more.

The arrival of Shinako's letter just then should have had the effect of fanning her jealousy; but, on the contrary, it served to dampen the explosion of emotion that was just about to occur. Had Shinako only kept silent, Fukuko would have insisted on settling once and for all the matter of Lily's unwelcome presence, which she felt she couldn't endure another day, by having her sent off to Shinako. But to hand over the cat now, after the other woman's attempt to stir up trouble with that insidious letter, was unthinkable—it would seem like giving in. In other words, Fukuko was caught between her resentment of her husband, and of Shinako: which emotion should she yield to? If she told her husband about the letter, it would seem as if she were allowing herself to be egged on by Shinako (though that was certainly not the case); so, rather than be made to look ridiculous, she'd keep it a secret. The question then was, who was the more hateful? Shinako's methods made her angry, of course; but her husband's behavior was unforgivable. Especially when she had to witness it with her own eyes day after day—it drove her wild. Besides, Shinako's warning—"Do be careful . . . or you may find yourself losing out to Lily in the end"—had had a greater effect on her than one might have thought. Of course, she didn't really believe for a moment that anything like that could happen; but if she could only chase Lily out of the house entirely, she wouldn't even have to worry about such silly things. On the other hand, for her to do that would give great satisfaction to her rival, which was an unbearable thought. When her hostile feelings toward Shinako gained the upper hand, she would decide it was better to put up with the cat rather than fall in with that woman's cunning schemes. And so, until she sat down at the dinner table this evening, she had been fretfully tossing about among these alternatives. But when she watched the usual game-playing and counted the mackerel as they vanished one by one from the plate, she suddenly lost control and decided it was her husband she should vent her anger on.

At first, she spoke merely out of spite, with no real intention of carrying out her threat to drive Lily from the house. It was mainly Shozo's attitude that complicated matters, and made the issue compelling. Since Fukuko had every reason to be angry with him, it would have been best for Shozo simply to agree to do as she wanted, without any fuss. If he'd shown his willingness to let her have her own way, she would have felt better at once, and perhaps not have insisted on her demand after all. But Shozo *would* try to excuse the inexcusable and evade the whole issue. It was a bad habit of his: he could not bring himself to say a clear "no" to anything. His strategy was at all costs to avoid upsetting the other person, to remain noncommittal until he was pressed to the wall; and then, at the critical moment, to shift positions. He would pretend to be about to agree to something, but never in fact say a firm "yes." He seemed timid, yet cunning and tenacious in his own way, too. Fukuko couldn't help noticing how, though he gave in to her on other things easily enough, when it came to Lily he'd try to pass it off by saying "What does it matter?—it's just a cat," while refusing to back down. Obviously his love for Lily was even stronger than Fukuko had imagined. The issue could not be left unresolved.

"Listen, Shozo...," she started in again that night, after crawling under the mosquito net. "Now, turn this way and listen!"

"Oh, I'm *so* sleepy ... just let me get some sleep...."

"No. Not till we settle this cat business."

"Does it have to be tonight? Wait till tomorrow...."

18

The light from the bulb hanging outside in the eaves cast a faint radiance through the curtains of the four full-length glass panels at the front of their shop, revealing the vague outlines of the furniture and objects within. Shozo had been lying on his back, the quilt pushed aside; but as he spoke he turned on his side, facing away from his wife.

"Don't you turn your back on me!"

"Please just let me sleep. A mosquito got inside the net last night and I couldn't sleep a wink."

"Well, then, will you do as I say? If you want to get to sleep, hurry up and decide!"

"God, you're mean. . . . Decide what?"

"Don't think you're going to fool me with that sleepy act of yours. Are you going to give Lily away or not? I want an answer right now."

"Tomorrow. . . . I'll decide tomorrow. . . ," said Shozo, as he began to breathe the deep, relaxed breath of sleep.

"Listen!" Fukuko sat up abruptly, turned toward Shozo, and gave his bottom a good strong pinch.

"Owww! What're you doing?"

"You!—always covered with scratches from Lily, and now you say a little pinch from me hurts?"

"Ouuuuch! Stop that!"

"Oh, this is nothing. . . . If that cat can scratch you, so can I— I'll scratch you from head to foot!"

"Owww! . . . Oh God. . . . Stop it!"

Shozo kept on shouting as he jumped up and tried to protect himself from his wife's attack. He was trying to keep his voice down, though, so as not to let his mother upstairs hear. Fukuko kept at it, now pinching, now scratching—there was no telling which it would be. Face, shoulders, chest, arms, thighs, everywhere—the attacks kept coming, and each time Shozo

19

dodged to avoid one, a dull thud resounded through the house.

"How's *that?*"

"Oh, please. . . . Please stop!"

"Are you awake now?"

"Yes, I'm awake. . . . Ouch! . . . That hurts!"

"All right, then. Give me an answer, yes or no."

". . . It *hurts!*"

Grimacing, rubbing various parts of his body, Shozo left the question unanswered.

"At it again, are you? Any more of your tricks and you'll get *this*," cried Fukuko, as she scratched his cheek as hard as she could with two or three fingernails. Shozo's pain this time seemed perfectly genuine, and his "Owww" had a tearful quality to it. Even Lily was shocked, and dashed out from under the mosquito net.

"Why're you putting me through this?"

"Ha! Since it's for Lily, you should *enjoy* it."

"Why're you still going on like that?"

"I'll go on as much as I want to, till you make up your mind. Now, are you going to get rid of Lily, or me—which?"

"Who ever said anything about getting rid of you?"

"Then you'll give Lily away?"

"It's not a matter of one or the other. . . ."

"Oh no you don't—you've got to decide."

Fukuko grabbed him by his shirtfront and began to poke him in the chest. "Well, which'll it be? Answer me . . . now! Right now!"

"Don't be so rough."

"I'm not letting you off tonight, no matter what. So let's have an answer—and make it quick!"

"All right, all right, have it your way. I'll give Lily away."

"You're sure?. . ."

20

"Yes, I'm sure." Shozo closed his eyes and assumed an earnest, resolute expression. "All I ask is that you wait one week. I suppose you'll get angry at me for saying this, but she's been in the family for ten years. You can't expect me to toss her out today, just like that—even if she is just an animal. Why not let her at least stay one more week, so I can give her her favorite food and do what I can for her—then I won't feel so bad about giving her away? Well, how about it? You could cheer up and be nice to her for that long, couldn't you? Cats can get nasty if you don't treat them right. . . ."

Shozo made his appeal with such apparent sincerity that she found it impossible to refuse: "All right, one week, then."

"Of course."

"Give me your hand."

"What?" asked Shozo; but before the word was out of his mouth Fukuko had seized his little finger and hooked it with her own, sealing the bargain.

"Mother. . . ."

One evening two or three days later, while Fukuko was at the nearby public bath, Shozo left the counter he'd been tending at the front of the house and went into the living quarters at the back, where his mother was eating her supper at her own small table. Bending down beside her, he began hesitantly: "Mother, I've got a little favor to ask."

His mother sat hunched over the table, eating her usual dinner of cold rice (boiled each morning almost to the consistency of gruel, then left in its earthen pot till mealtime) topped with salted seaweed.

"You see, all of a sudden Fukuko says she can't stand Lily, and she wants me to give her to Shinako. . . ."

"Yes, that was quite a racket you two were making the other night."

"Did you hear us?"

"In the middle of the night, thumping around like that?... Why, at first I thought it was an earthquake. Was it because of the cat?"

"Yes, and just look at this. . . ." Shozo rolled up his sleeves and held out both arms for her inspection. "Look, I'm a mass of scratches and bruises. See, there's even some here on my face."

"Why'd she do this to you?"

"Jealousy. It's crazy—says she's jealous because I'm too fond of Lily. Have you ever heard of such a thing? She must be out of her mind."

"But Shinako had things to say about that too, didn't she? Anyone'd be jealous, the way you carry on about that cat."

"Hmph!" Shozo had been used to being indulged by his mother since early childhood, and even now the habit persisted. He flared his nostrils like a spoiled child and said petulantly, "Oh, Mother, you *always* take Fukuko's side in everything."

"Now, Shozo, it doesn't matter whether it's a cat or a human being: if you pay too much attention to someone else and forget all about your brand-new bride, why, it's only natural she's upset."

"That's not it at all! I'm always thinking of Fukuko. She means more to me than anything."

"Well, then, why not let her have her way on a little thing like this?... I've heard all about it from her already."

"When was that?"

"She was talking about it yesterday. She said she can't stand having Lily around any more, and that you'd already promised to send her off to Shinako within five or six days. . . . Is that true?"

"Yes, well, I suppose I did. But that's what I wanted to talk to you about. Couldn't you kind of talk to her, and persuade her, so that we wouldn't actually have to go that far?"

"She says if you don't keep your promise, she'll leave."

"That's just a threat."

"Maybe so, but since she's so set on it, wouldn't it be better to agree to it? There's going to be trouble if you break your promise."

Shozo made a sour face, pursed his lips, and looked at the floor. He had counted on getting his mother to calm Fukuko down, but his calculations were going badly awry.

"With her temper, she just might run off, you know. That'd be all right, I suppose; but I can't have her father saying that he won't let his daughter stay here because the husband cares more about the cat than his bride! It puts *me* in a bad position."

"So you're also telling me you want me to get rid of Lily?"

"Just send her off to Shinako for a while, till Fukuko calms down a bit. Then you can bide your time and bring her back when Fukuko is in a better mood. That's the way to handle it, dear."

The old lady knew that once the cat had been given away, it was highly unlikely either that Shinako would ever agree to send her back or that Shozo would be allowed to accept her if she did. But just as Shozo liked to act the part of the pampered son, so too his mother continually tried to manipulate him, saying whatever seemed most likely to soothe him under the circumstances, humoring him like a difficult child. And, in the end, she always got this son of hers to do whatever it was she wanted.

She continued to wear an old-fashioned lined kimono with a sleeveless coat lightly padded with cotton for warmth, and knitted split-toed socks, at a time when young people were already beginning to wear serge. Thin and slight of build, she looked like an old woman whose vitality was completely spent; yet her mind was still sharp: she never made a slip in what she said or did. The neighbors used to say, in fact, that "the old lady does a lot better than her son." People were also of the opinion that it was she who was pulling the strings when Shinako was driven from the house, and that Shozo himself still had some lingering affection for his first wife. What with one thing and another, there were many in the neighborhood who disliked old Mrs. Ishii, and sympathy in general was with Shinako. To these criticisms, Mrs. Ishii responded that no matter how much a mother-in-law might dislike her son's wife, if the son was satisfied with her, she would never leave or allow herself to be driven out. If that had happened, it was, of course, because Shozo had got sick of her and her ways. And, certainly, that was true. Yet it was also an undeniable fact that, without the aid of his mother and Fukuko's father, Shozo would never have had the courage to drive his wife out all on his own.

Actually, Mrs. Ishii and Shinako had somehow failed to get along from the very first. The daughter-in-law, who had a strong, unyielding character, took care not to make any slips that would give occasion for criticism, and worked hard at serving her mother-in-law in the approved manner. Mrs. Ishii, however, was annoyed at this display of faultless behavior: "She doesn't *seem* to have any bad points in particular, but somehow I don't feel any warmth in what she does for me. . . . You see, she doesn't have a gentle, loving nature that really *wants* to make an older person's life a little pleasanter—that's why." The very fact that both mother- and daughter-in-law were such strong personalities led to disharmony between them. Still, for the first year and a half, things seemed to go well enough, at least on the surface. But then Mrs. Ishii started going off to stay with her elder brother (this uncle of Shozo's was named Nakajima and lived in Imazu) for two or three days at a time, on the grounds that she didn't enjoy her daughter-in-law's company. After she had been away for a while, Shinako would go to Imazu to see how she was, only to be told to "go back home and send Shozo to get me!" Then, when Shozo came, his uncle and his cousin Fukuko would join forces with his mother to make him stay on and on, even after nightfall. Shozo was vaguely aware that there must be some hidden motive in all this, yet off he went wherever Fukuko suggested—to a baseball game at Koshien Stadium, to the beach for a swim, to Hanshin Park. As he drifted along enjoying whatever pleasures came his way, he gradually found himself slipping into a very curious relationship with his cousin.

His uncle's business was the manufacture and sale of sweets; and, in addition to a small factory in Imazu, he owned five or six properties that he'd built to rent out, along the national highway. But, though he was very comfortably off, his daughter had become a real problem. Perhaps it was because she had lost her mother so early. At any rate, after she left secondary school in the middle of her second year (left, or was asked to leave), she had been unable to settle down. She ran away from home at least twice, and that fact had got into a Kobe newspaper, so her marriage prospects were slim. Besides, she herself wasn't interested in marrying into a stiff, respectable family. For all of these reasons, then, Nakajima was very eager to settle Fukuko's future somehow—a fact that Ishii O-rin was quick to notice. Fukuko was like a daughter to her; she knew what kind of a girl she was, and didn't care about the flaws in her character. Of course, it wouldn't do to have a daughter-in-law who was "loose," but she was now at an age when more discretion could be expected of her. Once she had a husband, she wasn't likely to be unfaithful to him—and even if she was, it wouldn't matter much. The point was that two of the rental properties along the national highway belonged to her, which meant an income of sixty-three yen per month. Since Nakajima had made the properties over to Fukuko some two years earlier, O-rin calculated that the accumulated earnings would amount to 1,512 yen, apart from interest. Fukuko would be bringing that much with her as a dowry, not to mention the regular sixty-three yen in rents. If you were to put all that in the bank, you would have quite a tidy sum after, say, ten years. This is what O-rin had in mind.

Of course there was no point in being greedy for her own sake, with only a few years left to her; but what about that feckless son of hers? How did he propose to get through the coming years? She wouldn't be able to die in peace, leaving that question unanswered. The old Ashiya road was less traveled with each passing year, now that the Hankyu railway had started operating and a new highway had opened up, so there was nothing to be gained by hanging on and trying to make a go of their kitchenware shop here. But to move somewhere else they would have to sell the present shop; and even supposing they could do that, she had no clear plan where to move to or what kind of business to set up. Shozo was by nature incapable of concerning himself with such things—he didn't particularly worry about being poor, and he wouldn't apply himself to business. When he was thirteen or fourteen he had worked as a messenger at a bank in Nishinomiya while attending night school; then he'd been employed as a caddy at the Aoki golf practice range. When he got a bit older he started as an apprentice cook. But nowhere did he last long; and while he was frittering away his time like this, his father died. Since then he had settled down as the owner of the kitchenware store—leaving all the work to his mother. Instead of looking for some sort of job like any other man, he talked about opening a "club-cafe" by the highway, and thought of having his uncle put up the money for it, until he was set straight. Apart from that, the only things he really wanted to do were raise cats, play a little billiards, fiddle about with potted *bonsai* trees, and flirt with waitresses at cheap cafes.

Then, about four years ago, at the age of twenty-six, he had married Shinako, who was working as a maid in a rich family's house in the Ashiya hills. Tsukamoto, the local tatami-maker, had acted as go-between. From the time of his marriage, the family business got worse and worse, and it became difficult to make ends meet from month to month. Since they had been living in Ashiya for two generations now, it was possible to put off payments of money owed the local shops for a time; but the monthly land rent of fifteen sen per four square yards had gone unpaid for close to two years and by now amounted to over a hundred and twenty yen. There was just no way they would be able to pay it. Shinako knew she couldn't count on Shozo for help and so tried to supplement the family income by doing sewing at home. And not only that—she even began selling off items of the trousseau she had scrimped and saved to buy out of her meager salary as a maid. Before long, most of the things were gone. After all that, it was really too cruel of them to try to drive her out—no wonder the neighbors' sympathies were all with her. But from O-rin's point of view, what had to be done had to be done; and the fact that Shinako was still childless after some years provided a convenient excuse. Fukuko's father, for his part, was pleased at the thought of his daughter finally settling down. And since it also allowed him to rescue his nephew's family from their financial plight—well, everyone seemed to benefit! Knowing he felt this way, O-rin was all the more determined to carry out her plan.

Thus both parents certainly played a part in the beginning of

27

the affair between Shozo and Fukuko. Still, even without paren-
tal encouragement, it might have happened, since Shozo was a
likable sort. He wasn't particularly good-looking, but there was
something childlike about him, even at this age, and he had an
easygoing disposition. As a result, the ladies and gentlemen who
came to the golf range were fond of him, and he got more in tips
and presents at the mid-year and year-end gift-giving seasons
than anyone else did. He was popular at the cafes too, and soon
learned the knack of enjoying himself in a leisurely fashion with
very little outlay. Inevitably, indolence had become a habit.

At any rate, O-rin had laid her plans with care and thus managed to land this nice young bride for her son, with a fine fat
dowry thrown in; so she and Shozo would have to do their best
to make sure that the young lady didn't fly off somewhere—
flighty creature that she was. In these circumstances, who cared
what happened to that cat? Besides, deep down, O-rin was sick
to death of the little beast. Lily had originally belonged to a
Western-style restaurant in Kobe where Shozo was working as a
live-in apprentice. When he quit that job, he brought her back
home with him; and how filthy the house had been ever since!
Shozo claimed that his cat never "made a mess," always using
her litter-box when Nature called. Well, wonderful—but she
made a point of coming home to use the box even when she was
out on the prowl. Naturally the thing stank and filled the whole
house with its nasty smell. Lily also had the habit of swanning
about the house with sand from her litter-box still clinging to
her hindquarters, leaving a gritty wake on the tatami mats of the
rooms through which she sailed. On rainy days especially, the air
in the house became close and the smell was very strong. And
on such days Lily would return from her walk outdoors, tracking
mud in from outside and leaving her footprints here and there.

Shozo also boasted of her cleverness in being able to slide

28

open doors, partitions, and paper screens, just like a human being. Open them she could; but, animal that she was, she failed to *close* them. So on cold days someone had to follow her about, closing each and every door, partition, and screen. Worse still, she left the paper screens full of holes and the wooden doors covered with scratches. Another sore point was that fish—raw, braised, or grilled—could not be left unwatched for any length of time without its being gobbled up. Even for the short time it took to set the table, any such food would have to be put into a cupboard or screened shelf. Worst of all, though, was the fact that while Lily had well under control what emerged from her rear end, the same did not hold true of the opposite end: she occasionally threw up. The cause was Shozo's passion for having her do acrobatics at the dinner table. He would keep tossing her tidbits until she was stuffed; then, when the table was moved after supper, one usually found lots of hair and half-eaten fish heads and tails scattered on the floor.

Yet, even though Lily and her habits had given O-rin a lot of trouble—and until Shinako joined the family it was Shozo's mother who did all the housework and cooking—she'd put up with it, because of something that had happened five or six years earlier. She had bullied Shozo into giving the cat to a grocer in Amagasaki; but one day, after a full month had passed, Lily had shown up at the house in Ashiya, having come back all that way on her own. Had she been a dog, there would have been nothing strange about this; but for a cat to have made the return trip of ten to fifteen miles out of love for her former owner was genuinely touching. As a result, Shozo's attachment to Lily became twice as strong as before, and even his mother seemed to sympathize. Or perhaps she had begun to feel that there was something uncanny about this particular cat; at any rate, she stopped trying to persuade Shozo to get rid of her. Then, after

Shinako came, Lily's presence became rather useful to O-rin as a means of getting at her daughter-in-law (Fukuko, of course, had had the same idea). In fact, O-rin even favored the cat with an occasional kind word.

So Shozo was stunned to see his mother now suddenly taking Fukuko's side in the argument over Lily.

"Well, but even if we do give Lily away, she'll come right back," he pointed out. "After all, she made it all the way from Amagasaki that other time."

"Yes, but this time she's not going to a complete stranger's, so who knows how she'll behave? And if she does return, we can always let her stay. Anyway, send her off for now...."

"Oh, what a mess—I don't know *what* to do." Shozo sighed several times and was about to try a new tack with his mother when suddenly there was the sound of footsteps from the street. Fukuko was back from the public bath.

"You do understand, Tsukamoto, don't you? You have to carry this as carefully as possible—don't swing it around any which way. Cats get car-sick too, you know."

"I know—I got you the first time."

"Oh, and there's *this*." Shozo held out a small, flat package, wrapped in newspaper. "It's the last time I'll be seeing her, you see, and I wanted to give her something really nice to eat, as a kind of send-off. But if I feed her just before she's taken away, it'll be very bad for her digestion. She loves chicken, so I went and bought some and boiled it for her. Now, when you get to Shinako's place, please be sure and tell her to give this to Lily right away."

"All right. And I'll take good care of her on the way, so don't worry.... Will that be all then?"

"Just a moment." Shozo opened the lid of the basket and lifted the cat out for one last cuddle. "Lily," he said, rubbing his cheek against hers, "mind you be a good little cat and do what you're told after you get there. She promised she wouldn't be mean to you like before. She'll love you and take care of you, so there's nothing to worry about. Okay?... Understand?"

Lily, who disliked being held anyway, pawed wildly in an attempt to escape from Shozo's too ardent embrace. Placed back in the basket, she poked and prodded about two or three times and then suddenly settled down, as if resigning herself to captivity. Watching her, Shozo felt even sadder.

He had wanted to see her off as far as the highway bus stop, but Fukuko had forbidden him to take one step out of the house for the next few days (except to go to the public bath). So, when Tsukamoto left with the basket, Shozo sat by himself in the shop, looking despondent.

His wife had forbidden him to leave the house because she was afraid that, in his anxiety about Lily, he might drift over to the neighborhood where Shinako lived, were he left to himself. And, to tell the truth, Shozo too felt much the same concern. Thus the unsuspecting couple began to sense Shinako's real motives only *after* they had handed over the cat.

Was that it? Was Shinako planning to lure him back, with Lily as the bait? If Shozo was found wandering in the vicinity of her house, did Shinako think she could somehow grab hold of him and win him back with her feminine wiles? The very thought filled Shozo with resentment at his ex-wife's cunning; at the same time, he felt all the more worried about Lily being used as a tool in such a plot. His only hope was that Lily might escape from Shinako's house in Rokko on the Hankyu line and come back home, as she had from Amagasaki some years before. Actually, it was with the thought that Lily might remember the route taken and so find her own way back that Shozo had asked Tsukamoto, busy with work after a recent flood, to make the effort to come in the morning rather than at night. Even now, Shozo vividly recalled that time long ago when Lily had returned from Amagasaki. It was at dawn one day around the middle of autumn that the slumbering Shozo was awakened by a familiar "meow, meow. . . ." He was single at the time, and slept upstairs while his mother slept on the ground floor. The shutters were still closed at this hour of the morning; but somewhere nearby a cat was mewing, and as Shozo listened, half asleep, it sounded uncannily like Lily. They had sent her off to Amagasaki a whole month ago, so how could she be here now? Yet the more he listened, the more it sounded like her. He heard the scratch and patter of paws on the tin roof outside his room at the back. . . . Now it was just outside his window. . . . He *had* to know. Leaping up from his quilts, he pushed open the shutters. There on the roof just in front of him, restlessly moving back and forth, was an extremely weary-looking but unquestionably identifiable Lily!

Shozo, hardly trusting his own eyes, called hesitantly: "Lily. . . ."

"Meow," she replied, looking up, her large, lovely eyes wide with happiness. She came to a point just below the bay window where he was standing; but when he reached out to lift her up, she slipped away, darting two or three feet in the opposite direction. She didn't go far, though, and at the sound of "Lily!" would give a "meow" and reapproach. Again Shozo would reach for her, and again she would slip from his grasp. It was precisely this aspect of a cat's character that Shozo loved. She *must* care for him, since she went to so much trouble to return. Yet, when she was safely back at her old familiar home and gazing up at the face of the master she hadn't seen for so many weeks, what did she do if he reached out for her? Run away. Perhaps, knowing his love for her, she enjoyed playing upon it like this; or perhaps she felt a bit awkward at their first meeting after such a long separation, and her shyness took this form. In any case, Lily kept on moving back and forth across the roof, replying with a "meow" each time Shozo called her name. Right away he noticed how thin she'd become, and as he looked more carefully he saw too that her fur had lost its sheen of a month before. Her head and tail were covered with mud, and bits of pampas grass stuck to her here and there. The grocer who had taken her in was known to be a cat lover, so it was unlikely he would have mistreated her in any way. No, Lily's pitiful state was obviously due to the "hardships of the road" she had suffered on her lonely journey back from Amagasaki. She must have walked all night to have arrived home at such an early hour—but it was certainly more than one night's journey. Night after night she must have walked, after fleeing from the strange house some days before. Losing her way, wandering down dark byways without knowing where they led, until at last she reached home. . . . The tufts of pampas grass proved that she hadn't come straight back along the highway, which was lined with houses and other buildings. How piercing the winds at dawn and dusk would have felt to a cat that, typically, disliked the cold. Besides, showers were common at that time of year, and she must have sometimes crept into thickets to escape the rain, or hidden in fields to evade pursuing dogs. She had been lucky to survive the journey.

Imagining all this, Shozo wanted to hold Lily and gently stroke her, and so he kept reaching out to catch hold of her. Gradually Lily, though seeming still a bit shy, began to brush her body against Shozo's outstretched hands, until at last she let her master have his wish.

Later Shozo learned that Lily had disappeared from the place in Amagasaki about one week before. Even now, years afterward, he couldn't forget the sound of her voice and the look on her face that morning. And there were many other memories: there was, for example, the day he first brought the cat home from Kobe. He'd just quit his last job as apprentice cook at the Shinkoken and returned to Ashiya. He was twenty that year; his father had died not long before, and the forty-ninth day memorial service was about to be held. Shozo had already kept a *miké* or "three-colored" cat in the kitchen of the restaurant and, when that died, a jet-black tom called "Blacky." Then one day the man from the butcher shop told him about a cute little female cat of a European breed, about three months old, that was available; it was Lily. When he quit the restaurant, Shozo left Blacky behind but couldn't bring himself to give up the new kitten. So he took her back to his house in Ashiya, carefully stowing her in a corner of a cart he had borrowed, together with his wicker trunk.

According to the owner of the butcher shop, the English called this particular type of cat a "tortoiseshell," and indeed the distinct black spots spreading with a lustrous sheen over the brown coat did resemble the polished surface of a turtle's shell. Certainly Shozo had never had such a lovely cat before, with such a magnificent coat. European cats are generally free from the stiff, square-shouldered look of Japanese cats; they have clean, chic-looking lines, like a beautiful woman with gently sloping shoulders. Japanese cats also usually have long, narrow heads, with slight hollows beneath the eyes and prominent cheekbones, but Lily's head was small and compact. Her wonderfully large and beautiful gold-colored eyes and nervously twitching nose were set within the well-defined contours of a face shaped exactly like a clam shell placed upside down. But it was not her coat or face or body that so attracted Shozo to this kitten. If it were only a matter of outward form, he himself had

34

seen Persian and Siamese cats that were even more beautiful. It was Lily's personality that was so appealing. When first brought to Ashiya, she was still terribly small, small enough to be held in the palm of one hand, but her wild tomboyish ways were just like those of a seven- or eight-year-old girl, a primary-school student at her most mischievous. She was much lighter than now and could jump to a height of three or four feet when her master held some food above her head during dinner. If he were seated, she could reach it so easily that he often had to stand up in the middle of his meal to make the game interesting. He began training her in such acrobatics from the moment she arrived. The morsel of food held at the end of his chopsticks would be raised little by little—three feet, four feet, then five feet—and each time Lily successfully made the jump. Finally she would leap onto Shozo's kimono at about knee height and nimbly crawl up his chest to his shoulder, then traverse his outstretched arm like a rat crossing a rafter, till she could reach the very tip of the chopsticks. Sometimes she would leap onto the curtains in the shop window and climb quickly up to just below ceiling level, cross from one side to the other, and then crawl down, again clinging to the curtains. Again and again she did it, revolving like a waterwheel.

From her kitten days she had a charming, lively expression; her eyes and mouth, the movements of her nostrils, and her breathing all showed the shifts of her emotions, exactly like a human being. Her large, bright eyes in particular were always roving about; whether she was being affectionate, or mischievous, or acquisitive, there was always something lovable about her. When she got angry, Shozo found her quite funny: small as she was, she would round her back and bristle her fur as cats do; her tail would rise straight up and, prancing and pawing the ground with her little feet, she would glare fiercely at her foe. It was like a child imitating an adult, and no one who saw her could keep from smiling.

Nor could Shozo forget Lily's gentle, appealing gaze when she first had kittens. One morning about six months after arriving at Ashiya, she started following Shozo around the house, mewing plaintively—she sensed she was about to give birth. He spread an old cushion in the bottom of an empty soft-drink carton and placed it at the back of the closet. Then he picked her up and carried her to her bed. She stayed in the box only briefly, soon opening the closet door and emerging to follow him about again, mewing all the while. Her voice was not the one he was used to hearing. It was still "meow," of course, but this "meow" had another, peculiar meaning to it. It sounded as if she were saying "Oh, what shall I do? I don't feel well, suddenly. . . . I'm afraid something very odd is about to happen to me. . . . I've never felt anything like this before! What do you think it could be? Am I going to be all right?. . . *Am* I?"

When Shozo stroked her head and said "There's nothing to worry about. You're going to be a mother, that's all," she placed her forepaws on his knee as if to cling to him, uttered one "meeoww," and looked at him as though trying her best to understand what he was telling her. Shozo carried her back to the closet and placed her in her box. "Now you stay right here, okay? You're not to come out. Okay? You understand?" Having made this little speech, he closed the door and started to stand up, when there was another plaintive "meeeoow." It seemed to be saying "Wait a moment. Don't go away." Shozo melted at the sound and opened the door just a crack to peek in. There in the farthest corner of the closet, which was filled with a jumble of trunks and cloth-wrapped bundles, was the box with Lily's head sticking out. "Meeooow," she cried, gazing at him. "She may be just an animal," thought Shozo, "but what a loving look she has in those eyes of hers!" It was strange, but Lily's eyes shining in the closet's dim recesses were no longer those of a mischievous little kitten. In that instant they had become truly feminine, full of an inexpressible sadness and seduction. Shozo had never seen a woman in childbirth; but he was sure that if she were young and beautiful, she would call to her husband with just the same pained, reproachful look as this. Any number of times he closed the closet door and began to walk away, only to go back for another look; and each time Lily would poke her head out of the box and peer at him, like a child playing peekaboo.

All this had happened as much as ten years ago, and Shinako had only appeared on the scene six years later. So, in the intervening period, Shozo had lived on the second floor of the Ashiya house with only this cat for company (apart, of course, from his mother). When he heard people with no knowledge of a cat's character saying that cats were not as loving as dogs, that they were cold and selfish, he always thought to himself how impossible it was to understand the charm and lovableness of a cat if one had not, like him, spent many years living alone with one. The reason was that all cats are to some extent shy creatures: they won't show affection or seek it from their owners in front of a third person but tend rather to be oddly standoffish. Lily too would ignore Shozo or run off when he called her, if his mother were present. But when the two of them were alone, she would climb up on his lap without being called and devote the most flattering attention to him. She often put her forehead against Shozo's face and then pushed as hard as she could; at the same time, with the tip of her rough little tongue she licked away at him—cheeks, chin, the tip of his nose, around his mouth—everywhere.

At night she always slept beside him and would wake him up

in the morning. This too was done by licking his face all over. In cold weather she would insert herself under the top quilt near Shozo's pillow and then work her way down into the bedding. She nestled against Shozo's chest, or crawled toward his groin, or lay against his back, wherever, until she found a place where she could sleep comfortably. Even after finally settling down in one spot, she often changed her position if it became the least bit uncomfortable. Her favorite posture seemed to be to lie facing Shozo, with her head on his arm and her face against his chest; but if he moved even a fraction her rest was disturbed, and she would burrow off in another direction, looking for a better spot. Accordingly, whenever she got into his bed, Shozo had to extend one arm as a pillow and then try to sleep in an obliging way, moving as little as possible. So positioned, he would use his other hand to stroke that area of the neck which cats most love to have fondled; and Lily would immediately respond with a satisfied purring. She might begin to bite at his finger, or gently claw him, or drool a bit—all were signs that she was excited.

Once when Shozo broke wind under the quilts, Lily, who was sleeping on top, toward the far end of the bed, awoke with a start and, thinking perhaps that some dubious creature with a very odd sort of voice was hiding there, began searching through the quilts in a great flurry, her eyes full of suspicion.

Then there was the time when Shozo tried to pick up an unwilling Lily: as she broke from his grasp and clambered down, she let fly with an evil-smelling fart which caught him full in the face. Admittedly, Shozo had by mischance clutched with both hands at Lily's belly, full to the bursting point with the meal she had just eaten. And unfortunately her anus at that point was situated just below his face, so that the "breath from her bowels" blew straight up at him. The stench was so bad that even a cat lover like Shozo was forced to toss her to the floor with an "Ugh!" The proverbial "weasel's last fart" must smell something like that. At any rate, it was an extremely stubborn smell which, once it clung to your nose, was not to be dislodged for the rest of the day, no matter how often you rubbed or washed or scrubbed away with soap.

Whenever Shozo had an argument with Shinako over the cat, he was apt to say sarcastically, "After all, Lily and I are so close we've smelled each other's farts!" But when you've spent ten years together, you do develop exceptionally strong ties, even with a cat. The odds were, in fact, that he really did feel closer to Lily than to either of his wives. As it happened, he had only been married to Shinako for a total of two and a half years, spread over four calendar years. And Fukuko had been in the household barely a month. Naturally, then, it was Lily, with whom he'd lived so long, who was more intimately bound up with many memories of his; who formed, in fact, an important part of Shozo's past. Wasn't it only normal to find the thought of giving her up after all those years painful? There was no reason for people to call him eccentric or cat-crazy, as if he'd completely lost his head. He felt ashamed of himself for having knuckled under so easily, for being so weak and helpless as to hand his dear friend over to someone else as if she meant nothing to him, just because of Fukuko's bullying and his mother's preachings. Why hadn't he tried to make them see reason, boldly and directly, like a real man? Why hadn't he been firmer, much much firmer, with both his wife and his mother? He might still have lost, and seen the same result, but by not having put up even that much of a fight, he had certainly failed in his duty to Lily.

Suppose for a moment that Lily had not come back after being sent off to Amagasaki. . . . That time, he had himself agreed to her being given to the other family, so he would have been resigned to it. Yet when he'd finally managed to catch Lily as she stood meowing on the tin roof that morning, and held her in his arms, rubbing his cheek against her, he'd thought, "What a terrible thing I did! It was downright cruel. From now on I'll never give her away to anyone, no matter what. . . . I'll keep her here to the end." He had not only vowed this to himself but felt that he'd made a firm promise to Lily as well. And now, when he considered how he had driven her out a second time, he was appalled at his own callousness.

What made it sadder still was that Lily had in the past two or three years clearly begun to age, the signs of decrepitude appearing in the way she carried herself, the look in her eyes, the color and condition of her coat. And no wonder: when Shozo first brought her home in that cart, he was still a youth of twenty; next year he would be almost thirty. In terms of a cat's life, ten years would probably be equivalent to fifty or sixty. So it was only natural that Lily should have lost her old vitality; and yet when Shozo—recalling as if it were only yesterday how the kitten would climb up to the top of the curtains and perform her tightrope act—looked at Lily now, scrawny-flanked, walking with head drooping and wobbling from side to side, he felt an indescribable sadness. It was if he were being given a personal demonstration of the Buddhist truth that "all things pass away."

There were many signs of Lily's rapid decline: one of them, for example, was her no longer being able to jump up with ease to Shozo's height and snatch a bite to eat. It didn't have to be food at mealtimes, either; any time she was shown something, she would make a leap for it. But each year the number of leaps grew fewer, and the height she reached lower. Recently, if she were shown a bit of food when she was hungry, she would first check to see if it was something she liked or not, and then jump; and, even so, it had to be held no higher than a foot or so above her head. If it were any higher she would give up the idea of jumping and either climb up Shozo's body or, when even that seemed too much for her, simply look up at him with those soulful eyes, her nose twitching hungrily. "Be kind to me. I'm starving, and I really do want to jump up and take that food. But at my age I just can't do it any more. So please, don't be mean; just toss it down to me—now." She made her wordless appeal as if knowing exactly how weak her master's character was. When Shinako got that sad look in her eyes, it didn't bother Shozo very much; but for some reason, when it was Lily, he was strangely overcome with pity.

She'd been such a charming and lively kitten—so when did her eyes begin to take on that mournful look? It must have been at the time she was about to give birth to her first litter, when she poked her head out of the carton in the corner of the closet and looked out helplessly at him. From that day on, her eyes were shadowed with a sadness which gradually deepened as she grew older. Looking into Lily's eyes, Shozo sometimes found himself wondering how it was that a little animal, no matter how clever, could have a gaze that seemed so full of meaning: was she really thinking sad thoughts at such moments? The cats he'd kept before, the three-colored one and Blacky, had never once had this sort of poignant expression—perhaps they were too stupid for that. Yet it wasn't that Lily had a particularly gloomy or melancholy temperament. When she was a kitten she was very tomboyish, and even after becoming a mother she could hold her own in a fight; she was a spirited cat, even a bit wild sometimes. But when she approached her master to be stroked, or lay basking in the sun with a bored look on her face, her eyes seemed full of a profound sadness. Sometimes they even became moist, as if with tears. When she was younger, that mistiness in her gaze seemed to have something voluptuous about it. But as she grew older, her bright eyes became cloudy, and mucus formed in their corners. Her sadness was so evident it was painful to see.

Perhaps this wasn't the way her eyes would naturally have looked, but was rather the result of the environment in which she'd been raised. After all, people's faces and characters often change when they've suffered a lot, and why shouldn't it be the same with cats? The more Shozo thought about it, the more guilty he felt toward Lily. For a period of ten long years he'd made her lead a lonely, dismal existence with only himself for company. Of course he had loved and cared for her; but when he had brought her home, it was just he and his mother living there, a far cry from the lively bustle of the Shinkoken's kitchen. And then, since his mother disliked her, Lily and he had had to share the lonely intimacy of a room upstairs. After six years had passed in this fashion, Shinako entered the household as his bride; and this intruder began to treat Lily merely as a nuisance, making her position still more uncomfortable and humiliating.

Shozo felt even guiltier about something else he had done. He should at least have let Lily keep and raise her kittens, but he'd adopted a policy of finding homes for them as soon as possible after their birth, so that not one remained in the Ishii house. Despite this, Lily kept on having kittens. She had three litters for every two of the average cat. Shozo had no way of knowing who her partner was, but the kittens were of mixed breed, and since they retained something of the look of a tortoiseshell, there were quite a few willing takers. Still, at times Shozo had to spirit some of them off to the seashore, or leave them under the pine trees on the Ashiya River embankment. It goes without saying that this was done out of concern for his mother's feelings; but Shozo himself believed that Lily's rapid aging might be due in part to her giving birth so often. If he couldn't prevent her from becoming pregnant, he could at least keep her from nursing so many kittens. It was from this point of view that he dealt with the matter. And, truly, Lily grew visibly older each time she had a litter. When Shozo saw her with her belly bulging like a kangaroo's and that mournful look in her eyes, he would say in a miserable voice, "You stupid cat. If you keep getting pregnant all the time, you'll be an old granny before you know it." If it had been a tomcat, he would have had it neutered, but the vet warned him that the same sort of operation was difficult with females. "Well, then, how about doing it with X rays?" The man just laughed at this suggestion. Everything Shozo had done was for Lily's sake; he'd had no intention of treating her unkindly. Yet it was undeniable that taking all of her offspring from her like that had turned her into a lonely, unfortunate cat.

Looking back, Shozo realized that he had put Lily through a lot. She had been a comfort to him over the years but had not had a pleasant life herself. Particularly in the last year or two, with quarrels between Shozo and his wife, and money troubles often creating household problems into which Lily was somehow always drawn, the cat had become demoralized, confused about her place in the family and uncertain what to do.

When his mother used to send for Shozo to come and take her home from Fukuko's house in Imazu, it was Lily rather than Shinako who tried to keep him from going, clinging to the skirts of his kimono with a pleading look. And when he shook her off and set out anyway, she followed along after him for a block or two, as a dog would. Shozo, in turn, would try to come back from Imazu as quickly as possible out of concern for the feelings, not of Shinako, but of Lily. If he had to stay away for two or three days, it seemed to him on his return that she looked even more forlorn than usual—or was it only his imagination?

Perhaps Lily was not long for this world. . . . The ominous

thought had often bothered him recently—he'd even seen her death in several dreams. Shozo himself appeared in them, sunk in grief as if he'd lost a parent, brother, or sister, his face wet with tears; and it occurred to him that, if he really did lose Lily, he would be just as heartbroken as in those dreams. And as one thought led to another, he felt frustration, shame, and anger all over again: how could he have handed her over so tamely? Sometimes he was sure he felt her reproachful gaze fixed on him from some corner or other. It was too late now for regrets, of course, but how *could* he have been so cruel as to drive that sad old creature away? Why didn't he let her die here at home, in peace?. . .

"Do you know *why* Shinako wanted the cat so badly?" asked Fukuko with an air of embarrassment, as she looked at her husband across the dinner table that evening. Shozo sat dejectedly sipping at his saké in the now strangely silent, desolate room.

"Hmmm. . . . I don't know. . . ," he replied, his face masked with incomprehension.

"She thinks if she has Lily, you'll come over to see her. That's it, don't you think?"

"Of course not. What a stupid idea. . . ."

"I'm sure that's it. It hit me today, for the first time. . . . And don't you be taken in by her tricks!"

"No, no, don't worry, I won't be."

"You're sure about that now?"

"There's no need to make such a fuss about it," said Shozo, giving a complacent little laugh and taking another sip of saké.

"Well, I'll have to be on my way—lots of work to do today." Tsukamoto placed the basket in the entrance hall and left. Shinako then carried it up the steep, narrow stairs and entered

44

the small four-and-a-half-mat room on the second floor that she had been assigned. She made sure the sliding door and glass window were shut tight, then set the basket down in the center of the room and opened the lid. Oddly enough, Lily made no immediate attempt to jump out of her cramped container. She craned her neck and began looking all around the room in a strange, wondering way. Only after some time did she venture out with slow, cautious steps and begin to sniff here and there, as most cats would in the same situation.

"Lily." Shinako tried calling to her two or three times, but received no more than a brief, cold glance in return. The cat went to the door of the room and to the closet and investigated their smells; then to the window, where she sniffed at each of the panes of glass, one by one. Then it was the turn of Shinako's sewing box, cushion, and yardstick, as well as some clothes she had begun to sew. Everything in the room was given the most thorough going-over. Meanwhile, Shinako remembered the parcel of chicken she'd just been handed by Tsukamoto and tried placing it, still in its paper wrapping, in Lily's path; but the cat seemed uninterested, giving it the briefest of sniffs before ignoring it. With the eerie, rustling sound that a cat's feet make on tatami, she completed her investigation of the room, then went back to the sliding door and tried to open it with her paws.

"Lily, you're *my* cat now and you mustn't run off somewhere!" Shinako blocked the exit, so Lily again began to pace the room, her feet making that curious sound. She went to the window facing north, climbed onto a box of scraps and swatches of cloth that happened to be there, and, stretching as high as she could, looked outside.

The day before had been the last day of September, and it was one of those bright autumn mornings. There was a slightly cold wind blowing, which made the leaves of the five or six poplar trees that stood in the vacant lot behind the house tremble, giving glimpses of their white undersides. Beyond them could be seen the peaks of Mts. Maya and Rokko. It was a very different view from the one upstairs in Ashiya, an area that was more crowded with houses. What could Lily have been feeling as she gazed at it? Shinako found herself recalling how often she and Lily had been left behind, just the two of them, in the Ashiya house. Shozo and his mother would both have gone off to Imazu, not to return for some time, and Shinako would be bolting down her lonely meal of hot tea over cold rice when Lily, drawn by the sounds of food being eaten, would come near. Oh yes, she'd forgotten to feed the cat—it must be hungry. Feeling sorry for the creature, she would put some of the tiny dried fish used for making stock on the remains of her rice and place it before her. Used to more elaborate fare than this, Lily gave no sign of being happy or grateful, and ate only the merest bit. Then Shinako would get angry, and any affection she was beginning to feel for the cat would vanish. When night came, Shinako spread the *futon* and waited for her husband, who might or might not be back that night. At the sight of Lily mounting Shozo's quilts and lazily stretching out full length, as if it were her right, Shinako felt something akin to hatred, and roughly rousted the sleeping cat and drove her off.

So she *had* vented her spite on the cat a good deal in the old days; yet here they were, sharing a room together again—perhaps, after all, they had some link from a former life. When Shinako had first settled in this second-floor room after being driven out of the house in Ashiya, she too had gazed at the mountains from that northern window, full of longing for her husband. So she could understand, in a way, how Lily felt now, looking out of the same window. Suddenly Shinako felt on the verge of tears.

"Lily dear, come over here and have some of this. . . ." She opened the closet door and took out the various things she had prepared. Tsukamoto's postcard had arrived the day before, so this morning she got up early and went to the dairy for fresh milk and then readied a few bowls and dishes, so as to be able to entertain her long-awaited and honored guest. Realizing that this particular guest would also require a litter-box, she had rushed out the previous night to buy a shallow pan. That was easy; but unfortunately she had no sand, so she'd gone to a construction site some five or six blocks away and, under cover of darkness, made off with some of the sand used in making concrete. This too was quietly stowed away in the closet.

Shinako took out the milk and a dish of rice with dried bonito shavings over it and a slightly cracked and chipped lacquer bowl. She poured the milk into the bowl and spread newspaper in the center of the room. Then she opened the packet from Shozo and set out the boiled chicken meat, in its bamboo-shoot sheath wrapping, together with the other delicacies. Finally she began calling, "Lilyyy . . . Lilyyy," clinking the dish against the milk bottle. The cat, however, remained pressed against the windowpane, pretending not to hear.

"Lily!" Now Shinako was getting excited. "What are you looking at out there? Aren't you hungry?" According to Tsukamoto, the cat had not been fed this morning because Shozo was worried she might suffer from motion sickness. If so, by now she should be begging to be fed; the first clink of a dish or bowl should make her come running. But, on the contrary, she seemed not even to hear the sound, or to feel hungry at all. Was she that eager to escape, then? Shinako had been told about Lily's celebrated return from Amagasaki, so she knew she would have to keep a sharp eye on her for a while. All she wanted, and had expected, was that the cat would eat and do her business in the litter-box.

If this was Lily's attitude from the very start, though, there was a good chance she really would run away. Now, Shinako knew that, in winning an animal's trust, patience is absolutely necessary; nonetheless, in her eagerness to see Lily eat something, she found herself dragging the cat from the window by force, carting her to the middle of the room, and then pushing her nose down over each of the waiting dishes in turn. Lily kicked wildly, put out her claws, and began to scratch, so Shinako had to give up and let her go. The cat returned to the window and climbed up onto the box of scraps.

"Lily! Look, here are all your favorite foods, can't you see?" Shinako stubbornly pursued the cat, going back and forth with the chicken, milk, and other things, pressing each one against Lily's nose. But today, at least, even the smell of her favorite dishes had no power over her.

It wasn't as if she had been given to a complete stranger, after all. The two of them had lived under the same roof and shared meals together for several years; sometimes they had been left alone with each other for three or four days, while the rest were off in Imazu. And now to be so cold to Shinako! Maybe she still resented Shinako for mistreating her occasionally. . . . But this only made the woman angry again. "Cheeky little thing!" If the cat did manage to run away, not only would all her careful plans have been in vain but, worse, those people in Ashiya would be clapping their hands for joy: "The joke's on her," they'd say. Anyway, it was a test of endurance she was now engaged in with the cat; there was nothing to do but wait till the other's resistance broke down. Why, with the food and litter-box set right in front of her, there was no way Lily could hold out. She was stubborn, all right; but she *would* get hungry, and she'd have to go to the toilet too.

But enough of this—it was going to be a busy day for Shinako since there was a bit of sewing that absolutely had to be done by this evening, and she hadn't touched it yet. Now, remembering, she went and sat beside the sewing box. She took up a man's padded silk kimono and set to work; but after barely an hour, she began to worry about the cat again and to steal occasional glances at her. Finally Lily moved to the far corner of the room and crouched there, pressed against the wall, motionless. It was as if, animal though she was, she knew there could be no escape and had given up even the thought of it. She seemed like a man who, hemmed in by some great sorrow, has cast all hope aside and resigned himself to death. It made Shinako uncomfortable to watch her, and at last she quietly went over to make sure the cat was still alive. She picked her up, checked her breathing, and tried poking her a bit. No matter what was done to her, Lily offered no resistance; but her body was tight and stiff to the touch, like an abalone's. What a stubborn cat she was! With things as they were, would she ever settle down and accept her new home? Perhaps she was putting on an act, watching for Shinako to let down her guard. She behaved as though she were resigned to her fate; but this was a cat who could, if need be, open a heavy wooden door on her own, so if she were left to herself she might well be able to slip away. Shinako began to feel that, as far as eating and excreting were concerned, it was not only Lily she had to worry about but herself as well. How could she go downstairs for meals, or even to the toilet?

When noon came and her younger sister, Hatsuko, called from the bottom of the stairs to tell her that lunch was ready, Shinako answered and rose to her feet. Then for a while she wandered restlessly around the room. Finally she tied three muslin waist-cords together and wound them around Lily, from shoulder to armpit and then crosswise to the other side. She wound and re-wound the long strip of cloth several times, to make sure it would

49

be neither too tight nor too loose, before tying a secure knot on Lily's back. Taking up the loose end, she began to walk around the room again until she hit on the idea of fastening it to a light-cord that hung down from the ceiling. Then, free from worry, she went downstairs.

During lunch, though, she became anxious again and, finishing as quickly as she could, went back upstairs to have a look. Lily, still trussed up, had made her way to the far corner, where she crouched, hunched down even smaller than before. Shinako had thought it might be better if she wasn't in the room for a while. Left to herself, Lily would eat her food and probably do her business as well. That was what Shinako was hoping for; of course nothing of the sort had happened. With a sharp click of her tongue, she went and sat beside her sewing box, glaring resentfully at the dishes of food pointlessly placed in the middle of the room, and at the immaculate litter-box, in whose sand there was not a trace of moisture. But it did occur to Shinako that it would be unkind to leave the cat trussed up like that for too long, so she got up and crossed the room to untie the cord. After doing so, she tried petting Lily, cradling her in her arms, and urging her to eat something (without much expectation of success). She also shifted the position of the litter-box. She went through the same motions any number of times, until finally it was dusk. Around six o'clock Hatsuko called from downstairs to say that supper was ready, and Shinako stood up, cord in hand. Thus the entire day was spent in dealing with the cat, and as the long autumn night drew on, she realized she still hadn't done her day's sewing.

At eleven, Shinako tidied the room and then tied up Lily. She put her to bed on top of *two* thick cushions and placed her food and litter-box nearby. She then spread her own bedding, turned out the light, and tried to go to sleep. But as she lay there, various thoughts ran through her head: if only Lily would *eat* something—a bit of chicken, a little milk, anything—by morning. . . . If she could open her eyes tomorrow and find one of the dishes empty, or the sand in the box just a little wet, how happy she'd be! As wishful thoughts like these kept Shinako wide awake, she strained in the darkness to hear Lily's breathing; but there was absolute silence, not one sound. It was so quiet, in fact, that it got on her nerves, and she raised her head from the pillow. There was a faint glow near the window, but unfortunately the corner where Lily should have been sleeping was pitch-dark. Suddenly remembering, she groped above her head and found the cord that was stretched diagonally from the ceiling. Giving it a tug, she was reassured—there was something at the other end. Just to make certain, though, she turned on the light. Yes, Lily was there all right, but her scrunched-down, hunched-over form looked as sulky as it had in the daytime. Her food and litter-box too were untouched. Shinako turned out the light in disgust. Soon she began to drowse off; and when, a little later, she awoke, the day had dawned. There, on top of the sand in the litter-box, was a large, unmistakable turd; and the dishes of milk and rice were completely empty. "Wonderful!" cried Shinako . . . waking from the dream.

Was it, then, really such a back-breaking task to win over a cat? Or was Lily a particularly stubborn case? If she were still an innocent little kitten, no doubt she'd come around easily. But an old cat was like an old human being—it was probably a terrible shock for it to be taken to new surroundings with different ways and customs. The shock might even kill it. Shinako had taken on the care of this cat, which she didn't even like, from a particular motive; she hadn't realized it would be this much trouble. She seemed doomed to suffer more than her share, even to the extent of losing sleep over an animal that had been, in a sense, her enemy in the past. Yet, when she thought of the link that bound them together, her anger faded; and she felt, rather, that both of them were to be pitied. After all, when she had first left the house in Ashiya to come here, she'd had a miserable time, spending her days alone and depressed in this small upstairs room. She had wept every day and every night, when her sister and brother-in-law weren't watching. She had had no energy for two or three days and had hardly eaten a thing. So it was only natural that Lily too should miss Ashiya terribly. After being loved and petted so much by Shozo, it would be positively ungrateful of her not to feel that way. And to be chased from your comfortable, familiar home and taken to live with someone you didn't really like, at Lily's age—it was bound to be painful. If Shinako really wanted to make Lily feel at home, she would have to consider her present feelings, and try to give her a sense of security and trust. Anyone would be upset if they were forced to eat when they were thoroughly depressed. Yet, by shoving the litter-box at her, Shinako had in effect said "If you're not going to eat, then at least piss, damn it!" It really wasn't very kind of her. And even if that could be overlooked, she had certainly gone too far in tying Lily up. If you want someone to trust you, you have to begin by showing trust in them. Lily could only have been more frightened after that—even a cat would hardly feel much like eating when all trussed up. Probably it made urinating more difficult, too.

From the very next day Shinako stopped tying the cat up. If she ran away, she ran away, and there was an end to it. From time to time she would leave Lily by herself for five or ten minutes; she still crouched stubbornly in her corner, but fortunately seemed to have no urge to escape. However, it turned out that Shinako had let her guard down too soon. It happened when she went downstairs for half an hour, thinking to enjoy a nice, leisurely lunch for a change. Suddenly she heard a sound from the second floor, and when she rushed back up to see, she found the sliding door open about five inches. Lily must have gone out into the corridor, passed through the six-mat room that faced south, and then jumped out onto the roof from a window that had, unluckily, been left open. There wasn't a trace of her now.

Shinako was on the point of giving a very loud shriek, but nothing came out. When she realized that all her painful efforts had been for naught, that in fact Lily had escaped, all thoughts of pursuit left her. She felt almost relieved, as if a burden had been lifted from her. Obviously she was no good at dealing with animals, and the cat would have run off sooner or later anyway; so perhaps it was best to get it over with right away. Actually, she felt more relaxed now, and no doubt her work would go more smoothly. She'd be able to sleep more easily at night too.

Even so, she went out to the vacant lot behind the house and searched here and there among the weeds, calling "Lilyyyy . . . Lilyyyy. . . ." But though she did this for a while, she knew in her heart that Lily wouldn't be wasting her time there in the back lot.

The night Lily ran away, and the next night, and the next, Shinako, far from enjoying a good night's rest, was unable to sleep at all. Perhaps because she was a temperamental woman, she often found it hard to sleep, despite being only twenty-six. When she was working as a maid, if something unpleasant happened, she just couldn't get to sleep; and for a long time after moving to her sister's house, she'd been getting no more than three or four hours' rest each night, probably because the room was new to her. At last, about ten days ago, she had begun to be able to sleep a little better. Why, then, had insomnia set in again, ever since that night? Was it because she was concentrating too much on her sewing, trying to catch up on the work she'd neglected on account of Lily? The long hours she was putting in left her shoulders stiff and her nerves on edge.

On top of everything else, Shinako was beginning to suffer from the cold, even though it was still only the beginning of October. She had always been sensitive to cold weather, and now her feet particularly bothered her; even after she got under the quilts, the chilly feeling hung on. She suddenly remembered how her husband's coolness toward her had begun. It was entirely due to her problem with the cold. Shozo, who slept disgustingly well, would be asleep within five minutes of getting into bed, only to be abruptly woken by the icy touch of Shinako's feet. It infuriated him, and he would order her to "sleep over there." Eventually, they got into the habit of sleeping separately, and in this their quarrels over the use of a hot-water bottle in cold weather also played a part. The reason was that Shozo's constitution was just the opposite of his wife's—he always felt twice as warm as the average person. His feet especially felt hot, and he claimed he couldn't sleep if they didn't protrude a bit from the bottom of the quilts, even in wintertime. So he hated getting into a bed that had been warmed with a hot-water bottle, and wouldn't stay put for even five minutes. Of course this wasn't the fundamental reason for the disharmony between the two; but, all the same, the undeniable differences in their physical makeup provided a good excuse for husband and wife to sleep apart.

Shinako was now suffering from a terrible stiffness that spread from the right side of her neck down to her shoulder. She tried massaging the sore area, switching from sleeping on her right side to her left, and changing the position of her pillow. Every year during the change of seasons from summer to fall she was bothered by pain from a bad tooth in her lower right jaw, and beginning last night she had felt a few twinges. Indeed, she had heard that Rokko was far colder than Ashiya in winter, with the winds blowing straight down from the mountains. Even now, in October, the nights were quite cold, so although the two towns were located in the same general area between Osaka and Kobe, Shinako felt as if she had come to some distant mountain country. Curling up like a shrimp, she rubbed her feet, slightly numb from the cold, together. In her Ashiya days she had begun warming the bed around the end of October (even if it meant quarreling with her husband); but with weather like this, she might not be able to wait till then this year. . . .

Giving up any hope of getting to sleep, Shinako switched on the light and picked up last month's copy of *The Housewife's Friend*, which she'd borrowed from her sister. As she turned on her side and began reading, she noticed it was exactly 1:00 A.M. Shortly afterward she heard the steady sound of rain, first approaching from some distance, then passing directly overhead. "Oh, a shower," she said to herself, as more rain drew near. As it passed over the house, there was a pattering on the roof, which gradually faded away. Then the rain came on again. But where was Lily now, Shinako wondered. . . . If she'd made it back to Ashiya, that was fine; but if she had lost her way and was caught by the rain on a night like this, she'd be soaked to the skin. Shinako had not yet actually informed Tsukamoto of Lily's disappearance, and it had been weighing on her mind ever since that night. She knew of course that it would have been better to let him know sooner; but she had put it off, vexed at the thought of the slightly sarcastic response she could expect from him: "Excuse me, ma'am, but Lily's been back for some time now, so you don't need to worry yourself any longer. You've gone to a lot of trouble over her, and I suppose you won't be needing her any more now."

On the other hand, if Lily had gone back to Ashiya, surely they wouldn't have waited for word from Shinako, but would have contacted her from their side by now. Yet there had been no message, so perhaps Lily was wandering lost somewhere. It had taken her exactly one week to get back from Amagasaki, but Rokko wasn't nearly as far from Ashiya as Amagasaki was, and she'd been brought there only three days before, so she shouldn't have lost her way. Only, Lily's age had begun to tell on her recently: she was not as quick-witted as she had been, and her movements were slower. It might well take her four days now to make a journey she used to do in three. Even so, she should arrive safely back in Ashiya by tomorrow or the next day at the latest. Then just think how happy those two in Ashiya would be—and how they'd gloat! Why, Tsukamoto himself would probably join in the chorus: "Now look at that. Not only was she jilted by her husband, but by his cat too!" Oh yes . . . and no doubt her sister and brother-in-law would be thinking the same thing, down there on the first floor. In fact, everyone who heard about it would—she'd be a laughingstock.

The shower passed over the roof again with its patter of rainfall, and then there was a sudden thud, of something bumping against the window. "The wind's come up. Oh, Lord." But just as the thought crossed her mind, something that seemed a bit too heavy for it to be the wind banged twice in succession against the glass, and Shinako heard a faint "meow" from somewhere. Surely not now, at this time of night . . . it couldn't be. . . . Startled, and thinking it must be her nerves, she strained her ears. "Meow." There it was again; and, right afterward, another bang against the window. Shinako jumped up and rushed to open the curtain. Now she clearly heard a "meow"

56

from just outside; and with another loud bang a shadowy black something flitted by. Was it true, then?... Could it really be so?... She knew that voice. She hadn't heard it even once during Lily's stay with her in this second-floor room, but she remembered it well from the days in Ashiya.

Hurriedly unlocking and opening the window, she leaned out and scanned the dark rooftop by what light there was from the overhead lamp in her room. For a moment everything was blackness. She supposed that Lily had climbed onto the small half-balcony with its railing and, meowing, knocked at the window. That would account for the banging sound and the fleeting black shadow a moment ago; but as soon as the window was opened from inside, the cat must have run off somewhere.

"Lilyyyy...," Shinako called out into the darkness, taking care not to wake the couple downstairs. The roof tiles were wet and gleaming, so she had been right about the shower of a few minutes before; yet the clear night sky with its twinkling stars made it seem unreal now. On the broad, pitch-black flanks of Mt. Maya, which rose directly before her, the lights of the cable car had long since been extinguished, but some light could be seen in the hotel perched on the summit. Placing one knee on the low balcony, she leaned precariously out over the roof and called "Lilyyyy ..." again. There came a "meow" in reply, and two glowing eyes moved slowly across the tiles in Shinako's direction.

"Lily!"

"Meow."

"Lily!"

"Meow."

Again and again she called her name, and each time Lily answered. This had never happened before. The cat seemed to know who was really fond of her and who felt a secret dislike;

thus, when Shozo called, she always answered, but Shinako she completely ignored. Tonight, however, not only did she take the trouble to answer any number of times, but her voice gradually became extraordinarily sweet and coquettish. She would come directly under the railing, looking up at Shinako with her greenish, glowing eyes and swaying a little from side to side; then slip some distance away. No doubt that particular tone of voice was meant partly as an apology for past rudeness to a person she herself hadn't much liked but whose favor she was hoping for from now on. The cat was determined to make Shinako understand that she'd had a complete change of heart and was now looking forward to enjoying the lady's patronage and protection.

As for Shinako, she was as happy as a child at receiving such gentle, friendly responses from the cat for the very first time. But, though she kept on calling to her, every attempt she made to catch hold of her ended in failure. She decided to move away from the window for a while to see what would happen, and, sure enough, Lily at last leapt nimbly into the room. Then, to Shinako's utter astonishment, she walked straight over to her as she sat on the bedding and placed her forepaws squarely in the woman's lap.

What could this mean?. . . As Shinako sat there amazed, Lily looked up at her with a gaze full of sadness and, pressing herself against her breast, pushed with her forehead at the collar of the woman's flannel nightgown. Shinako found herself rubbing her cheek against Lily's head; and before long the cat started licking at her chin, her ears, the tip of her nose, around her mouth— everywhere. Shinako had heard people say that when a cat was alone with its owner, it would sometimes kiss and rub its face against that person, showing its love in much the same way as humans do. Was this what they were talking about? When

Shozo was off enjoying himself with Lily where no one could see them, was this what they were doing? Shinako smelled the peculiar, dusty odor of cat fur and felt all over her face the prickly, tickling friction of a cat's rough tongue against her skin. She felt a sudden surge of love and, crying "Lily," held her tightly in her arms. In the midst of her emotion, though, she noticed something gleaming cold and wet here and there on Lily's fur. Ah, so she did get caught in that rain just now. . . . Now Shinako understood.

All the same, why did Lily choose to come back here, rather than go to Ashiya? Presumably she was heading for home when she escaped, but then lost her way and so turned back. To wander for three days trying to reach a place less than ten miles away only to give up and come back seemed awfully feeble for a cat like Lily; but perhaps the poor thing had become that decrepit. Her spirit may have been as strong as ever, which was why she made her escape; but with her senses of sight and smell and her memory functioning at only half their former levels, she wouldn't have been able to tell how she'd been brought from Ashiya, which roads she'd taken, from what direction. Wandering hither and thither, completely lost, she must at last have decided to turn back. In the old days, if she had made up her mind to get somewhere, she would have plunged ahead, come hell or high water. Now, however, her confidence was gone; and if she entered an area she didn't know, she lost her nerve and her legs began to tremble. Probably, then, Lily hadn't been able to get very far after all, and had been hanging about the Rokko area for some time. If so, she could very well have been hiding somewhere near Shinako's second-floor window . . . last night, the night before . . . peering in, wondering if she should ask to be taken in again or not. No doubt she had spent a good long time crouched there in the darkness tonight, thinking about it, and had decided to let out that meow and knock at the window because the light in the room had suddenly been turned on just as it began to rain.

At any rate, it was *good* that she had come back. Of course she'd done so because of the difficulties she'd encountered, but at least it showed she didn't regard Shinako as a total stranger. And wasn't it a kind of sixth sense that had made Shinako herself switch on the light and read a magazine at such an unusually late hour on this particular night? Not only that—her inability to sleep for the past three nights must have been due to some vague sense that Lily would return. This thought made the tears come, and she gave the cat another tight hug: "Oh, Lily, Lily. . . . You mustn't go away again, ever!" Throughout all this, the cat remained unusually quiet, apparently content to be hugged for as long as Shinako desired.

The woman felt that she could now tell to an uncanny degree what this silent old cat with her melancholy eyes was feeling.

"I know you're hungry, but it's too late tonight. If I rummaged around in the kitchen, I suppose I could find something; but it's not my house, you see, so you'll just have to wait till tomorrow morning."

With each word, Shinako rubbed her cheek against Lily's head; then at last she set her down and closed the window, which in her excitement she had forgotten to do. She piled cushions for a bed and took from the closet (where it had sat unused since that terrible night) Lily's litter-box. All this time Lily was following her around, entwining herself between Shinako's legs. If the woman stood still even for a moment, Lily ran to her and, bending her head to one side, rubbed the base of her ear against Shinako's calf.

"Yes, yes, I know. . . . Now come over here and go to sleep. . . . That's right," Shinako crooned as she carried Lily to her cushions. Then she hurriedly turned out the light and crawled into her own bed. Within less than a minute, though, she smelled that familiar odor of dusty fur somewhere near her pillow; and a soft, velvety, furry thing began silently working its way under the top quilt. Lily pushed with her head, burrowing down to the foot of the bed where she roamed about for a while before climbing back up. Putting her head inside the breast of Shinako's nightgown, she stopped moving, and after a while began to purr, very loudly and happily.

Ah yes—Shinako had often heard just this sort of purring from Lily while in Shozo's bed; lying to one side, listening to it, she had felt intensely jealous. If the purring seemed louder than usual tonight, did that mean Lily was in an especially good mood? Or was it just that it *sounded* louder when it was right next to you in your own bed? Feeling Lily's cold, wet nose and the curiously soft and puffy pads of her feet against her breast now for the first time, Shinako's reaction was mixed—it felt odd, yet made her happy. Fumbling in the darkness, she began to stroke Lily's neck, at which the cat purred even louder and occasionally gave a sudden little bite to the tip of Shinako's index finger, hard enough to leave teeth marks. Although she'd never experienced this before, she knew it was a sign of intense pleasure and excitement.

From the next day it was clear that Lily had become fast friends with Shinako and trusted her from the heart. Milk, dried bonito shavings over rice—everything, in fact, was consumed with pleasure; and several times each day the cat's droppings appeared in the sand of the litter-box. As a result, the four-and-a-half-mat room was always filled with an unpleasant odor, but Shinako found that it revived in her various unexpected memories. She felt as if the good old days in Ashiya had somehow returned. It was only natural: the air in the house there had been heavy with this same smell from morning to night. Every sliding screen, pillar, wall, and ceiling in that house was permeated with it. Hadn't she spent close to four years together with her husband and mother-in-law, putting up with all sorts of irritating and painful things, and breathing in this same smell all the while? And yet, though at the time she had cursed the awful stink of it, what sweet memories it now brought back to her! Then, she had hated the cat in part because of the smell; now, she loved it all the more for the same reason. From this point on, Shinako slept with Lily in her arms almost every night and asked herself how she could ever have hated this lovely, docile little creature. The woman she had been came to seem to her now a very mean and nasty sort of person—a real monster, in fact.

It is necessary to say a few words here about Shinako's motives for sending that disagreeable letter concerning the cat to Fukuko and then pressing the matter so insistently via Tsukamoto. To be perfectly honest, there *was* an element of malice and sheer pleasure in making trouble, as well as the faint hope that Shozo might pay a visit to Rokko, drawn by Lily's presence. But her real purpose was connected not with these immediate prospects and pleasures, but with something much further down the line: in half a year, perhaps, or one or two years at the latest, Shinako foresaw serious trouble between Shozo and Fukuko. Her own marriage to Shozo had been a mistake, into which she'd been led by Tsukamoto's persuasive words as go-between. Now, when she considered what a lazy, good-for-nothing, weak-willed man he was, she realized it may have been all to the good, being cast aside by someone like that. If, even so, she felt humiliated and unable to resign herself to what had happened, it was because she knew that the two of them, man and wife, had not grown tired of each other but that a third party had successfully schemed to drive her out. Yet if she came right out and said this, Tsukamoto and others would think, even if not directly say to her, that it was her vanity speaking: "Of course it's true that relations between you and your mother-in-law weren't perfect," she imagined them saying, "but then things weren't going all that well with your husband either, were they? You said he was an idiot, and treated him like a backward child; he said you were selfish and domineering, and that you depressed him. Watching the two of you quarrel all the time, anybody could tell you'd never get along. Anyway, if your husband really loved you, he wouldn't have taken another woman on the side, no matter how much he was pushed by some 'third party.' "

But if people said or thought that, it was because they didn't understand Shozo's character. As Shinako saw it, if he were pushed hard enough by that "third party," he would have no choice in the matter. He was easygoing—perhaps "spineless" would be the better word: if someone told him this person was better than that one, he would readily go along with it. But he certainly wasn't the type to find himself a new woman and then get rid of his present wife—he didn't have that much gumption. Shinako had had no illusions that he was madly in love with her, but then again she had never felt disliked either; so if the people around him hadn't put the idea into his head and set the whole thing in motion, her marriage would never have broken up. All her troubles were due to scheming arrangements on the part of O-rin, Fukuko, and Fukuko's father. Deep inside her there smoldered a feeling of resentment at having had her marriage virtually hacked apart. A more mature person might have re-signed herself to what had happened, but Shinako simply could not let things stand as they were.

But if she felt so strongly, why couldn't she have done some-thing about it at the time when, as she vaguely sensed her-self, O-rin and the others were beginning to act?... Or why didn't she at least put up more of a fight when she was finally on the verge of being kicked out? People said she should be a good match for her mother-in-law when it came to plotting and plan-ning: why, then, did she just furl her flag and quietly leave without a struggle? It wasn't at all like her usual, stubborn self.

However, she had motives of her own for acting as she did. The truth was, she found herself in her present situation be-cause at first she had been a bit too careless. She had underes-timated the danger to her marriage, assuming that O-rin never really intended to accept this oversexed former juvenile delin-quent as a wife for her son; and feeling sure as well that fickle, "easy" Fukuko would not put up with a man like Shozo for very long. Though she may have been a little off in her calculations, her view that the two of them wouldn't stay together long was unchanged. Of course Fukuko was young and had the kind of looks men liked. She had no real education to boast of, but she *had* attended a girls' secondary school for a year or two. Most im-portant of all, she would bring with her a considerable dowry. Shozo could hardly be expected to throw down his chopsticks at this carefully prepared feast; and no doubt he would consider himself a very lucky man, for a while.

But Fukuko would soon discover that Shozo could not satisfy her, and would lose no time in finding others who could. No, Fukuko was certainly not a one-man woman; she was already notorious for that, and things would be no different now. When it became too obvious, even easygoing Shozo would have to say something, and O-rin herself would be forced to give up on her. Even if Shozo was blind to all this, surely O-rin, with her reputation for shrewdness, could not have failed to see what would happen. Greed, however, had played a big part in O-rin's thinking on this subject, so she may have felt compelled to do whatever was necessary.

Shinako decided it was pointless to put up what would almost certainly be a futile struggle; it seemed better to let her enemies win this one battle, and then quietly lay plans for the future. She had by no means given up; but she was careful not to breathe a word of her real feelings even to Tsukamoto. Outwardly, she tried to appear miserable, so that everyone would sympathize with her, while in her heart she was determined to get back into the Ashiya house again, no matter what. She'd show them all! It was this hope that kept her going through everything.

In addition, it must be admitted that, though Shinako thought Shozo completely unreliable, she couldn't bring herself to hate him. Incapable of deciding things for himself, he wavered on, turning now to the right, now to the left, according to what the people around him said. In this business, too, he was obviously being manipulated by that bunch. When she looked at it in this way, she couldn't help feeling sorry for him, and concerned—it was like watching a toddler trying to walk on his own. And, after all, there *was* something basically innocent and childlike about him. If you thought of him as a normal male adult, his behavior was often infuriating; but handle him like someone not quite on your own level, and the mild, agreeable, charming side of his nature came to the fore. Shinako had found herself helplessly bound up with him in this kind of relationship, and had poured into it every item of value she had brought with her in her trousseau. Then she'd been tossed out, after being virtually stripped naked. It was because she had done so much for the Ishii household that she was so full of resentment. Hadn't she for the past one or two years provided more than half the income for the family, "weak woman" though she was? Fortunately for them all, she was good with a needle and thread and had taken in sewing from the neighbors. Working far into the night, she had managed somehow to tide them over. Without her work and income, what would O-rin have done, for all her lofty airs? O-rin was disliked throughout the neighborhood, and certainly no one who knew his character trusted Shozo, so the local shopkeepers would have clamored for payment of the mass of overdue bills. Only people's sympathy for Shinako and her difficult position allowed the Ishiis to make it through the season for settling bills at the end of the year.

And yet that ungrateful mother and son, the pair of them, blinded by greed, had dragged in a woman like that! No doubt they thought they'd been very clever, exchanging their dumb ox for a fine-looking horse; but let them just wait and see whether that woman could run the household properly. Bringing a dowry with her was all well and good, but it would probably make her even more selfish and willful as a wife, while Shozo would get even lazier with her income to count on. In the end all three members of the new family would be disappointed, and this would give rise to endless quarrels. Then Shozo would at last recognize the real worth of his previous wife: "Shinako was never sloppy like this. . . . Remember that time when she did such-and-such, or that other time when she did so-and-so? . . ." And not only Shozo—why, even O-rin would come to admit her mistake and regret what she'd done. As for that other woman, after throwing the household into total confusion, she'd just up and run off. It was clear to Shinako that that's how the sorry tale would end; she could guarantee it. And to think that the Ishiis couldn't see it—some people were so blind! Laughing scornfully to herself, she had made up her mind simply to wait. At the same time, prudent as always, she thought of hedging her bets by keeping Lily with her as she waited.

In terms of formal education, Shinako had always felt a bit inferior to Fukuko, who'd at least had the advantage of a year or two of secondary school. But if it came to a true test of wits, she was confident she could beat either Fukuko or O-rin; and when she came up with the idea of getting hold of Lily, she was really quite pleased with her own cleverness. For if she had Lily, she was sure that when Shozo thought of the cat, he would also, unavoidably, think of her; and his pity for Lily would unconsciously turn into sympathy for Shinako as well. Thus a kind of emotional link would be maintained; and when his relations with Fukuko began to sour, his thoughts would turn with love and longing to Lily, which also meant to his former wife. Hearing that she had still not remarried and was leading a lonely life with only the cat for company, most people would feel sorry for her; and Shozo too could hardly take it amiss. This would probably reinforce his dislike of Fukuko; and so Shinako, without doing a thing, would succeed in breaking up their marriage and hastening her own remarriage to Shozo. . . . . Well, it would be wonderful if things worked out so perfectly for her—and she, at least, expected that that's the way it would be. The only problem was whether the people in Ashiya would meekly hand over the cat. Shinako was confident that everything would be all right, however, if she could simply fan her rival's jealousy a bit. The letter she had sent Fukuko was therefore written with great care and calculation; it wasn't just an exercise in spitefulness or troublemaking. Those poor fools in Ashiya, though, couldn't begin to understand her real reasons for asking for a cat she didn't even like. When she thought of them making a great, childish fuss about it, and bothering their heads with silly theories and suspicions about her motives, she felt an irrepressible sense of her own superiority.

Since that was the way things stood, her disappointment when the precious cat ran away and her delight when she unexpectedly returned were equally intense; and essentially these reactions would seem to have stemmed from Shinako's well-calculated long-term strategy rather than from any real affection for Lily. Yet their life together there on the second floor since the night of the cat's return had produced some very unexpected results. Night after night, as she lay in bed with this furry little creature in her arms, Shinako would be amazed at how genuinely lovable a cat could be and wonder how she could have failed to realize it in the old days. The thought troubled her conscience and filled her with remorse. In her Ashiya days, she had conceived a dislike for the cat from the very beginning, which made her blind to Lily's charms. The reason for her dislike was of course jealousy; because of that, Lily at her most winning seemed merely hateful. She hated the cat for crawling into her husband's bed on cold nights, and resented Shozo for allowing it. Yet when she thought back on it now, she realized there was nothing to hate, nothing to resent. Hadn't she herself been suffering a lot from the cold lately, sleeping alone? A cat, having a higher body temperature than a human, would obviously be even more sensitive to the cold. They say cats suffer from the heat only on the three hottest days in midsummer. Wasn't it perfectly natural, then, that an elderly cat like Lily would be drawn to the warmth of someone's bed in the middle of autumn? And, more to the point, how wonderfully warm the bed seemed to Shinako herself, now that she was sleeping with Lily. In other years, she would have been unable to sleep without a hot-water bottle by now; but this year she felt not the slightest bit cold, and had no need for one—and all thanks to Lily! Night by night, the prospect of doing without her was becoming more unthinkable.

Before, Shinako had also disliked Lily for her self-centeredness, for changing her attitude depending on whom she was dealing with—in short, for being two-faced. But all of that was due to her own lack of love. Cats have a wisdom of their own—they understand at once how someone feels about them. Lily's behavior proved it: as soon as Shinako changed her attitude and began to feel real affection for her, the cat came right back and behaved in the most friendly way possible. Hadn't Lily in fact sensed the change in Shinako's feelings more quickly than she herself had?

Shinako knew that she'd never felt or shown such tender affection toward anyone till now—not to a human being, and certainly not to a cat. One reason was that O-rin and other people had told her so often that she was hardhearted, she had come to believe it herself. But when she considered how much trouble she had put herself to recently for Lily's sake, she was surprised, wondering where these warm and gentle feelings had been hiding all this time. She remembered how amazed she used to be to see Shozo doing everything for the cat himself: planning her daily meals; going to the beach to get fresh sand for the litter-box every two or three days; brushing her and looking for fleas whenever he had spare time; always alert for any signs of a dry nose, or a watery stool, or loss of fur. If there was the slightest abnormality, the appropriate medicines were administered. Watching him being so attentive, Shinako would get more and more bad-tempered: "Look at that lazybones rushing around taking care of his cat!" Yet now it was she who was doing all these things for Lily. Moreover, she was doing them in someone else's house. She had agreed to pay her sister and brother-in-law for the cost of her own meals, so she wasn't in the humiliating position of a total dependent; still, she was keeping the cat in an environment where she herself didn't feel completely at home.

If it had been her own house, she could have foraged in the kitchen for leftovers to give Lily; but here it was impossible, so she either had to save her own food for the cat or go to the market especially to get something for her. Her situation required that she be extremely frugal, and even the small sums expended on Lily's food involved real sacrifices on her part. The litter-box presented another problem. The house in Ashiya was only five or six blocks from the sea, so it was easy to get sand; but Rokko, on the Hankyu line, was far from the coast. The first two or three times, Shinako was able to collect some sand at a construction site nearby, but recently, alas, no ready supply of this sort had been available. If she left the sand unchanged, however, the smell was dreadful, even penetrating to the first floor, which made her relatives unhappy. So she was obliged to sneak out of the house late at night, shovel in hand, and scrabble around in the nearby fields for earth, or steal the sand at the bottom of the children's slide in a local grade-school playground. On nights like these, she often had to contend with barking dogs and strange men who seemed to be following her. But since it was for Lily's sake, she willingly put up with it, though nothing else could ever have induced her to do things as distasteful as this.

Over and over she asked herself why she couldn't have shown even half this much love for the little creature when she was in Ashiya. If only she had made the effort, probably her marriage would not have broken up, and she would never have had to go through all this misery. How deeply she regretted it all now. She realized that it was no good blaming anybody else—it was she who had been at fault. Her husband had come to hate her because she was the sort of woman who couldn't even love a sweet, innocent animal like this. And the "third party" had been able to take advantage of this great failing of hers.

When November came, it was appreciably colder at dawn and dusk, with the winds that sometimes blew down from Mt. Rokko at night penetrating the house through cracks and crevices around the doors. Shinako and Lily pressed closer together and clung tightly to each other as they slept, trembling from the cold. Finally, unable to endure the chill any longer, Shinako began to use her hot-water bottle—to Lily's great delight. Every night the woman lay in her quilts, lovely and warm from both the hot-water bottle and Lily's body, and listened to the cat's contented purring. She would bring her mouth close to the cat's ear as she lay curled at her breast and whisper: "You've been much more loving than I have, haven't you?. . ."; or, "Now you're lonely too, and it's my fault. . . . I'm sorry, Lily. . . ."; or, "But it'll be only a little while now. Put up with this for just a bit longer and you'll see—we'll both be able to go back to Ashiya, together. And this time the three of us will get along fine. . . ." If the tears began to come, though there was no one but Lily to see her in that pitch-dark room in the middle of the night, she would quickly draw the top quilt up till it covered her head.

When Fukuko announced that she was going to visit her family in Imazu and left the house a little after four in the afternoon, Shozo, who had been pottering about with the orchid plants on the back veranda, stood up as though he'd been waiting for this chance and called out "Mother—" in the direction of the kitchen. His mother was doing the washing and apparently couldn't hear him because of the splashing and scrubbing, so he called out again in a louder voice "Mother! . . . Take care of the shop for me, will you?. . . I'm going out for a bit."

The splashing and scrubbing sounds abruptly came to a stop, and her firm voice was heard from beyond the paper screens:

"What'd you say?"

"I'm going out for a bit."

"Where to?"

"Just close by."

"What for?"

"Do you *have* to ask all these questions?" For a moment Shozo flared his nostrils and assumed a petulant expression. Then, as if thinking better of it, he said in his more characteristic good-little-boy tone of voice:

"You don't mind if I go and play a little billiards for thirty minutes or so, do you, Mother?"

"But didn't you promise not to play billiards?"

"Oh, come on, just this once. . . . I haven't gone for over two weeks now. . . . Come on . . . please."

"I don't know whether you should or not. Ask Fukuko about it when she gets back."

"But *why?*"

His mother, squatting by the washtub at the back of the house, could tell from the oddly blustering tone that her son was angry, and she formed a clear picture of the pouting, spoiled-child look on his face.

"Why do I have to ask my wife every time I want to do anything? Can't you tell whether something's right or wrong without asking Fukuko?"

"Yes, of course I can; but she particularly asked me to keep an eye on you. . . ."

"Then you're spying for her!"

"Don't be silly."

72

She paid no more attention to him and went on with her vigorous washing and scrubbing.

"Are you *my* mother, or Fukuko's? Which is it? Hunh? Which?"

"Now stop that. Shouting like that, do you want the neighbors to hear?"

"Well, then, leave the washing till later and come here for a second."

"All right, all right, I'll keep my mouth shut. Go wherever you please—I don't care!"

"Now, don't talk like that, Mother. Just come here for a second, will you?"

What *was* he thinking of? Shozo suddenly ran to the kitchen entrance where she was still crouched by the drain and, taking her by a wrist that was covered with soapsuds, virtually dragged her along to his part of the house.

"Here. This is a good chance for me to show you something."

"What're you making all this fuss about?. . ."

"Take a look at *this!*"

Shozo opened the closet door in the inner six-mat room that served as his and Fukuko's living room, to reveal a large pile of red material crammed into a dark space between a wicker trunk and a chest of drawers placed in a corner at the back.

"What do you think that is?"

"That?. . ."

"It's all Fukuko's dirty laundry. She shoves her things in there, one on top of the other. She never does any washing, so the dirty things just pile up there, and now you can't even open the drawers in that chest!"

"That's strange. . . . I always send her things out to the laundry, so—"

"But surely you don't send out her undies!"

73

"Ohhh. Are those . . . undies?"

"That's right! Why, just look at how sloppy she is—and her a woman! It's shocking. I bet you noticed too, but you never say a word to her. You're after me all the time; but when it comes to Fukuko, you pretend not to notice, no matter what she does. Isn't that so?"

"How could *I* know there were things like this shoved in here?. . ."

"*Mother!*" Shozo cried out in amazement despite himself. O-rin had crawled into the closet and started pulling out pieces of dirty laundry.

"What are you doing?"

"I thought I'd just tidy up a little, dear."

"Stop that! They're filthy. Stop it right now!"

"Never you mind, dear. Just leave it to me."

"What is this? A mother-in-law picking up her daughter-in-law's dirty undies? I'm not asking you to do that, Mother; I'm asking you to make Fukuko do it!"

O-rin acted as though she hadn't heard him. Taking five or six round red bundles of English flannelette from the dim depths of the closet, she carried them to the kitchen entrance, using both arms to do so, and put them in the washtub.

"Are you going to wash those for her?"

"Don't you worry about it—this isn't a man's business."

"Why won't you let her at least wash her own underwear—will you tell me that, Mother?"

"Oh, be quiet! I'm just putting them in the tub to soak. When Fukuko notices them here, she'll get the idea and wash them herself, I'm sure."

"That's *stupid*. She's not the type to 'notice.' "

Despite what she said about Fukuko washing the things later, Shozo was sure his mother intended to do it for her, and the thought made him all the more upset. Without bothering to change out of his rough work clothes, he scuffed into a pair of wooden-soled sandals in the entranceway, hopped on his bicycle, and was off.

He was telling the truth when he'd said earlier that he wanted to go and play billiards; but now he felt so irritable that he didn't give a damn about it any more. Ringing the bell on his bicycle furiously, he set off without any particular destination in mind, going straight along the path by the Ashiya River in the direction of the new national highway. After he crossed Narihira Bridge, he turned his handlebars toward Kobe. It was still a little before 5:00 P.M., but where the highway vanished in the distance, the late autumn sun was already beginning to set. A thick band of rich color stretched across the western horizon, and the sun's rays fell almost parallel to the surface of the road. People and cars alike were bathed in a reddish light and cast immensely long shadows behind them as they passed. Shozo was facing straight into the sun as he rode along, so he was forced to turn his head away and look down to avoid being blinded by the glare of the paved road, which shone like steel. He passed in front of the public market at Mori and was nearing the Shoji bus stop when suddenly he caught a glimpse of Tsukamoto, the tatami-maker, hard at work sewing a mat that lay on a low platform before him, just outside the walls of a hospital beyond the railway tracks. Shozo pedaled over to him, looking more cheerful than he had up to then.

"Are you busy?" he asked.

"Oh, hello there," answered Tsukamoto, glancing at him without stopping his work. He plied his needle as if he were determined to finish the job before sunset, stabbing it sharply into the tatami, then yanking it out again.

"Where're you off to at this hour?"

"Oh, nowhere special. I just came over this way. . . ."

"Was there something you wanted to talk to me about?"

"No, nothing really." Shozo was startled at his own answer; but it was too late now, so, with an ambiguous, forced smile which produced a few uneven wrinkles on his brow, he continued: "I was just passing, so I decided to say hello. . . ."

"I see." Tsukamoto immediately looked down and went on sewing, as if to say he really couldn't be bothered with this fellow standing there in front of him with his bicycle. Now, from Shozo's point of view, no matter how busy he might be, it wouldn't have hurt Tsukamoto to ask "How've you been lately?" or "Have you got used to not having Lily around any more?" or something of the sort. He felt mortified. After all, he was doing his best to hide his longing for Lily from Fukuko: he wouldn't allow even the "Li" of "Lily" to pass his lips in her presence. His almost limitless affection had, then, to remain pent up inside him; and when he ran across Tsukamoto by chance like this, he honestly expected to find him a sympathetic listener whom he could unburden himself to, and so obtain some comfort and relief. Didn't Tsukamoto realize that he ought at least to say a few consoling words to Shozo, or at any rate to apologize for not having been in touch with him since that day? Because in the first place, when Shozo agreed to hand Lily over to Shinako, Tsukamoto had made a solemn promise to go and visit the cat occasionally on his behalf, to find out just how she was being treated. He was supposed to take stock of the situation in Rokko and then report back to him. This was of course a private agreement between the two of them, kept strict-ly secret from O-rin and Fukuko. It was only on this condition that Shozo had been willing to let go of his precious Lily; and yet not once had Tsukamoto kept his promise! He just took advantage of a person and then pretended to know nothing more about it.

Or maybe he wasn't playing the innocent, but was simply too caught up in his everyday work to notice other people's feelings. Shozo felt an urge to put this chance meeting to good use and give the fellow a piece of his mind. But it was hard to bring up, quite casually, the topic of his cat with someone working busily away right there in front of him. And if he did manage to, wasn't there a good chance that it was he who'd get yelled at rather than the other way around, as it should be?

As the light gradually faded around him, Shozo stood there with a blank look, apparently fascinated by the large needle in Tsukamoto's hand—the only thing that glittered as it caught the remaining light. There weren't many houses in the area, even though it was by the national highway. To the south was a pond where frogs were raised for eating, while to the north there was only a large stone "Highway Jizo"; this Buddhist guide of the souls of the dead was brand-new, having just been erected in memory of people killed in traffic accidents on this road. Behind the hospital were a number of rice fields, and far beyond them rose the mountains that stretched along the Hankyu line. Until just a little while before, their many-layered folds had been distinct beneath a clear blue sky; now a thin, gray, twilight mist was beginning to conceal them.

"Well, then, I'll be going. . . ."

"Drop over sometime. . . ."

"I'll be over soon, when I have more time." Placing one foot on the pedal, Shozo took two or three awkward steps and then came back, as if he just couldn't resign himself to leaving things as they were: "Look, sorry to bother you, but actually there *is* something I meant to ask you."

"Oh? . . . What?"

"I was thinking of going over to Rokko now. . . ."

Tsukamoto, who was just standing up after finishing one tatami, dropped it back onto the platform with a thud and said, in astonishment:

"To do what?"

"Well, after all, I've no idea how she's been doing since then, you know. . . ."

"Are you serious? Act like a man—leave her be!"

"You don't understand, Tsukamoto. It's not that way at all."

"That's why I told you at the time to think it over carefully. And you said 'I won't miss that woman a bit. It makes me sick just looking at her.' "

"Now, hold on, Tsukamoto. It's not Shinako I'm talking about —it's the cat."

"The *cat*, you say?" A smile suddenly appeared around the tatami-maker's eyes and on his lips. "Ohhh, the cat. . . . I see."

"That's right. You remember, don't you?—you promised to go over once in a while to see if Shinako's taking good care of her."

"Did I say that? Well, anyway, I've been real busy this year, what with all the flood damage, so—"

"Oh, I know; that's why I'm not asking you to go over there for me."

This remark was meant to be quite sarcastic, but the hearer didn't seem to notice.

"You still can't forget about that cat, eh?"

"How could I forget about her? Ever since you took her away I've been worried sick. Is that Shinako mistreating her? Has Lily got used to it over there? I even have nightmares about it. And I can't say a word about it in front of Fukuko, which just makes me feel worse and worse—here. . . ." Shozo struck himself on the

78

chest and barely managed to suppress a sob. "To tell the truth, I wanted to go and see for myself at least once before now, but for the last month or so they've hardly ever let me go out alone. Besides, I don't like the idea of having to meet Shinako. . . . Do you think there's some way I could just slip in and see Lily, without Shinako knowing anything about it?"

"I think that'd be difficult." Tsukamoto laid his hand on the tatami resting on the platform, as if to say he'd had quite enough of this conversation. "You'd be sure to be seen. And if people thought it wasn't the cat you'd gone to visit, then you'd be in real hot water."

"Oh, I wouldn't want anybody to think that."

"So just forget it. Once you've given something away, that's the end of it, no matter how you feel about it. . . . You see that, don't you, Ishii?"

"Listen," began Shozo, not replying to Tsukamoto's question but introducing a new topic. "Does Shinako spend her time on the second floor, or the first?"

"Second floor, I think; but of course she comes downstairs too sometimes."

"Doesn't she ever leave the house?"

"I don't know. . . . She does some sewing work, so I suppose she's mostly at home."

"What time does she go to the bathhouse?"

"I wouldn't know."

"I see. . . . Well, sorry to have bothered you."

"Ishii!" Tsukamoto found himself addressing the rear end of Shozo's bicycle, which had traveled some three or four yards just in the time it took the tatami-maker to lift his handiwork from the platform and rise to his feet. "Are you really going there?"

"I don't know what I'm going to do yet, but anyway I'll go

over to the neighborhood and take a look."

"It's up to you, but don't come running to me if there's some problem later."

"And don't you say anything about this to Fukuko or my mother, all right?"

Then Shozo crossed to the other side of the tracks, his head swaying from side to side.

But would he really be able to bring it off as he hoped—avoiding all contact with the members of the household in Rokko and yet managing a private meeting with Lily? Fortunately there was a vacant lot behind the house, with tall weeds and poplar trees offering places to hide in; he would just have to wait patiently until Lily came outside. Unfortunately, however, it was already so dark that it would be difficult to spot her even if she did emerge. Also, Hatsuko's husband could be expected back from work soon, and the kitchen would be busy with preparations for the evening meal, so he couldn't hang about the vacant lot forever like a burglar on the prowl. Maybe it would be best, then, if he came back another day, at an earlier hour. But whether he could actually see Lily today was of secondary importance to Shozo now; what he really enjoyed was the chance simply to go wherever he liked without his wife's knowledge for the first time in quite a while. If he let this opportunity slip, it would be perhaps two weeks before he had another. Fukuko regularly went to her father's place to squeeze some pocket money out of him, but that was generally only twice a month, around the first and the fifteenth. When she went, she was always asked to stay for supper, which meant she wouldn't be back in Ashiya till eight or nine o'clock at the earliest. Today was one of those days, so Shozo knew he could enjoy another three or four hours of freedom. If he were willing to put up with hunger and cold, he could afford to stay at least two hours in that empty patch of land. So perhaps he would be able to meet Lily there after all, assuming she still kept to her old routine of going out for a stroll after supper. Yes, and he remembered now—she liked to find a spot where there was grass growing and eat some of the green blades after her meal; so the vacant lot looked all the more promising as a meeting place.

These were his thoughts as he rode past the Konan School and stopped in front of the Kokusuido radio shop. He peered inside and made sure the owner was there before opening the glass door about halfway and offering a friendly "Good afternoon."

"I'm awfully sorry," he went on, "but I wonder if you could lend me twenty sen."

"Will twenty sen do?" The shopkeeper recognized Shozo, of course; but he looked doubtful, as if he wanted to say that the two of them weren't close enough to warrant this sudden appearance and casual demand for money. Still, he could hardly refuse to lend him such a small sum, so he took two ten-sen coins from his portable cashbox and, without any further comment, put them in Shozo's outstretched hand. The young man promptly ran across the street to the Konan marketplace and bought a bag of bean-jam buns and a parcel wrapped in bamboo sheaths, which he placed in his breast pocket.

"Do you mind if I use your kitchen for a bit?" he said, on returning to the radio shop.

Now Shozo seemed a good-natured person, but he had no scruples about imposing on other people. He was used to making requests like this, so when the shopkeeper asked "What for?" he simply answered "I need to do something," grinned at the man, and headed for the kitchen. Without unwrapping the packet of chicken meat, he put it into an aluminum pan full of water, lit the shopkeeper's gas burner, and proceeded to boil it. Then, with twenty or so thank-yous and awfully-sorrys, he went on to ask for the loan of a lamp for his bicycle: "I hate to keep bothering you, but do me this one last favor, will you?"

"Sure, take this along," said the man, bringing out from the back of the shop an old paper lantern from some caterer's, with the words "Miyoshi-ya of Uozaki-cho" inscribed on it.

"Wow, that's a real antique!"

"I don't really need it. You can return it any time it's convenient."

Since it still wasn't pitch-dark outside, Shozo set off with the lantern stuck into his sash. When he came to a large signboard with the words "Path up Mt. Rokko begins here," in front of the Rokko stop on the Hankyu line, he left his bicycle at a tea shop on the corner and climbed the not very steep slope that led to the house he was looking for, some two or three blocks further up. Going around to the north side, behind the house, he entered the vacant lot and sat crouched on his heels in a thick clump of grass and weeds about two or three feet high, holding his breath in anticipation.

Shozo's plan was to wait there patiently for, say, two hours, munching on the bean-jam buns he'd brought with him. If Lily appeared, he'd give her the chicken as a special treat, and then perhaps enjoy a little cuddle with her—have her jump up onto his shoulder and lick him around the mouth—for the first time in weeks.

He would have worn an overcoat if he'd known where the quarrel with his mother would lead him today; but he had left home in a hurry, and it was pure chance that had made him take the road west and bump into Tsukamoto, which resulted in his coming this far. With only a woolen undershirt beneath his thick cotton work clothes, he really felt the cold. He hunched his shoulders and looked up at the night sky, which by now was filled with glimmering stars. Cold blades of grass brushed against his bare feet in their wooden-soled sandals; he touched his shoulders and the top of his cap and realized that a heavy dew was falling. Well, no wonder he felt so chilly! If he stayed squatting here for two whole hours, he'd probably catch cold. . . . But the smell of fish being grilled came wafting from the kitchen, and Shozo felt sure that Lily could smell it too and would appear from somewhere or other at any moment. He felt a strange tension as he began to call out in a small voice, "Liiiily . . . Liiiily." He tried to think of some signal he could give that would be understood only by the cat, and not by the people in the house.

In front of the clump of weeds where he was crouching, there was an arrowroot plant covered with leaves, from the midst of which came an occasional gleam of some sort. Presumably it was a drop of dew or something, reflecting the light from a distant lamp. But even while acknowledging this, Shozo's heart leapt within him at each gleam, hoping that it might be the glow of Lily's eyes: "Is that her? Wouldn't it be *wonderful!*" He could feel his heart beating faster at the thought, and a kind of chill in the pit of his stomach; but the next moment would bring disappointment.

Odd as it may sound, Shozo had never experienced this sort of agitation and impatience before, even in his relations with other human beings. Fooling around with cafe waitresses was all he'd been capable of. The closest he had come to a love affair was when he was seeing Fukuko on the sly, hiding it from Shinako. Yes, that pleasant, vexing, oddly exciting, and unsettled feeling had been his nearest approach to love. Even so, his mother and Fukuko's father had quietly guided the two of them through it all and put up a good front toward Shinako, so there had been no need for him to go to unreasonable lengths—none of this squatting in the chill evening dew and sustaining himself with bean-jam buns! And for that very reason, his affair with Fukuko had always lacked a certain seriousness: never had his desire to see her or meet her been anything like as intense as his feelings for Lily were now.

Shozo was aware that both his mother and his wife treated him like a child, a rather backward child who would never be able to make it on his own; and he was very unhappy about it. But he had no friend he could air his grievances to; and as he was forced to keep them bottled up, he came to feel somehow lonely and helpless. This made his love for Lily all the greater. Those lonely feelings that neither Shinako nor Fukuko nor even his mother could understand—it was only Lily, with those sad eyes of hers, who could pierce through to them and offer comfort. And Shozo was sure that he was the only one who could read her sorrow, the unhappiness that the cat had deep within her but couldn't express directly to human beings. It was over forty days now since the two of them had been separated from each other. At first, it was true, he had tried not to think about it and to resign himself to her absence as quickly as possible. But his resentment toward his mother and his present wife kept building up, and there were fewer and fewer outlets for his pent-up anger. The result was that his longing for Lily reared its head again and would not be suppressed. Given Shozo's position, it was natural that all the interference with his comings and goings, the strict seclusion that was enforced on him, should have the effect of fanning his love for the absent cat. Even had he wanted to forget her, he was given no chance to do so.

Another source of worry was the fact that he had heard nothing at all from Tsukamoto. Why, after making all those promises, didn't he get in touch? If he was too busy with his work, then it couldn't be helped; but perhaps that wasn't it at all—what if Tsukamoto was hiding something from him, trying to keep him from worrying? Maybe Shinako had been treating Lily badly, and she was now in a terrible state, suffering a breakdown of some kind. . . . Or she might have run away and be completely lost, whereabouts unknown. . . . Maybe she became ill and died there in Rokko. Who could tell? Ever since Lily had been taken away, these were things Shozo had often dreamed about. He would wake up with a start in the middle of the night, think he heard her meowing somewhere nearby, and, pretending to go to the toilet, quietly get up and open the shutters. After he'd been taken in by these phantoms a number of times, he began to wonder, with a shiver of fear, if the voice he heard and the figure he saw in his dreams might not belong to Lily's ghost. Had she fled from Rokko and then died somewhere by the road-side, leaving only her spirit to make its way back to its master's house?

Yet, no matter how spiteful Shinako was or how irresponsible Tsukamoto might be, surely they wouldn't remain silent if something awful really had happened to Lily. After all, the fact that there was no news was proof that all was well! Each time any unlucky thoughts suggested themselves to Shozo, he kept on denying them like this. And, despite his worries, he'd had another reason for faithfully following his wife's orders not to visit Rokko: apart from being strictly watched, he was determined not to fall into the trap Shinako had set for him. He wasn't sure even now just what her real motive had been in taking Lily; but he suspected that Tsukamoto's failure to report to him might have been due to a suggestion on her part: she may have hoped to make him so anxious that he would be lured into coming to Rokko. And though he wanted somehow to make sure that Lily was all right, he'd be damned if he'd let that crafty woman get him in her clutches.

Just imagining the superior, knowing look he was sure she would put on—"Ah, so finally you're here!"—filled him with loathing. But Shozo too had always had his own type of cunning, which took the form of a skillful use of the appearance of weakness—his seeming to be the sort of person who would do whatever others told him. It was this that had allowed him to get rid of Shinako: outwardly, he seemed just a puppet in the hands of O-rin and Fukuko, but in fact he detested Shinako more than all the rest of them ever could. Even now, he felt that he'd done the right thing, that she had it coming to her; he didn't feel the slightest trace of pity for her. And right this minute she was probably there in that room beyond the window on the second floor, where the light was on. As he crouched among the weeds, looking up at the light, that mocking, know-it-all face of hers flashed before him, arousing more feelings of disgust.

After coming all this way, he wanted at least to hear Lily's sweet "meow," even if only from a distance, before he went back to Ashiya. Just to know she wasn't in any trouble would bring him some peace of mind and make the trip worthwhile. And, taking things a step further, if he were to creep up to the kitchen entrance and take a peek inside. . . . With a bit of luck, perhaps he could call Hatsuko out for a little chat in private, give her the chicken meat he'd brought, and learn from her how Lily had been getting on. . . . But these pleasant thoughts were brought to a halt by the sight of that light in the window, and the thought of that face. Shozo began to go weak at the knees. If he wasn't careful, Hatsuko might get the wrong impression and actually summon her sister from the second floor. And at the very least she was bound to tell her about it afterward. "Well, my plan is beginning to work," Shinako would say in her self-satisfied way. No—he wasn't having any of that!

So he would have to continue squatting patiently in this vacant lot, waiting to seize his chance when Lily happened by. On the other hand, since he'd waited this long already without results, it was tempting to give up. He had eaten all the bean-jam buns in his bag. Besides, he was sure an hour and a half had already passed, and he was beginning to worry about what would happen back in Ashiya. If it was just his mother there, it wouldn't be a problem; but if Fukuko returned before he did, he'd never be allowed to go to bed and would end up covered with bruises. More alarming still was the thought of being kept under even stricter supervision from then on.

Anyway, it was strange that not once during the hour and a half he'd been waiting here had the faintest sound of meowing come from the house. Was it possible that the nightmares he'd been having so often lately had come true, and Lily was no longer here? If the fish he had smelled grilling a little while before had in fact been for the family supper, Lily would surely have been given something at the same time; and when she'd finished eating, she would come out to nibble on some grass. But she *hadn't* come out, which seemed very odd....

At last Shozo, unable to bear it any longer, rose from the clump of weeds and stole toward the door in the back fence. Pressing his face to a chink in the wooden door, he could see that the shutters on the first floor had been closed. The sound of Hatsuko's voice as she apparently put her children to bed came to him in snatches; apart from that, there was nothing to be heard. If only he could catch a glimpse of Lily's shadow against the panes of that second-floor window, how happy he would be! But, beyond the glass, all he could see was a white curtain hanging motionless, its upper part less brightly lit than below. Shinako must have lowered the overhead lamp as she did her night's work. Shozo imagined the peaceful scene: the woman busily sewing in the lamplight and Lily quietly curled up beside her, fast asleep. In the long autumn night, the steady lamplight held Lily and her, just the two of them, in its warm circle, leaving everything else in the room as far as the ceiling dimly obscured.... As the night deepened, the cat began to snore faintly while the woman went on with her silent sewing—a forlorn but touching scene....

If that was the world hidden behind that window—if, by some miracle, Lily and she had become the best of friends—if Shozo was actually shown the scene he had just imagined—would he be able to fight down a feeling of jealousy? To tell the truth, if Lily had completely forgotten about the past and was quite content with her present situation, it would make him angry. On the other hand, if she were being abused, or if she were dead, he would feel even worse. Since he would feel bad in either case, perhaps it would be best after all to learn nothing....

Suddenly he heard the clock on the first floor strike the half hour: "Bong...." It was half past seven. The realization made him start, as if someone had given him a sudden push. He took two or three steps away from the fence, then came back and took out the packet of chicken he'd been keeping carefully hidden inside his clothes, and began wandering about with it, from the wooden door to the garbage can, back and forth. He wanted to leave it in a place where only Lily would find it: if he put it in the weeds, some dog would probably sniff it out, and if he left it right here, someone in the family would see it. Wasn't there some way he could—no, he had no time to worry about this now. If he didn't make it home within thirty minutes at the latest, there'd almost certainly be another row. "And just *where* have you been till this hour of the night, mister?" He could hear Fukuko's voice even now, as if she were right beside him, and he could see the look of rage on her face. Hurriedly he opened the packet and put it among the arrowroot leaves; he placed pebbles on top of the open bamboo wrapping, on both sides, and then arranged some of the leaves over it as cover. Then he ran as fast as he could across the vacant lot and back to the tea shop where he had left his bicycle.

That evening, Fukuko, who had returned about two hours after Shozo did, was in an extremely good mood as she told the Ishiis about taking her younger brother to a boxing match. And the next day, finishing supper a little earlier than usual, she announced "We'll be going off to Kobe for a bit"; and husband and wife set out for the Jurakukan, an entertainment area in Shinkaichi.

In O-rin's experience, Fukuko was always in a good mood just after staying with her father—that is, for the five, six, or seven days she had her father's money in her pocket. During this period, she spent as much money as she pleased, usually treating Shozo to a movie or a musical a couple of times at least. As a result, the two of them got on extremely well for a while, like any loving couple. But after about a week had passed and most of her money was gone, Fukuko would begin to laze about the house doing nothing except snacking and reading magazines; and then she'd occasionally start in on her husband, when she thought he needed it. And Shozo, on his side, would act the part of the faithful, loving husband only so long as his wife was in funds. When the money ran out, there was a notable change in attitude: his replies became halfhearted and his manner rather listless. The one at a real disadvantage at these times was O-rin, who was drawn into her son's and daughter-in-law's quarrels from both ends. Naturally, then, every time Fukuko ran off to Imazu, O-rin felt immensely relieved, knowing that there would be peace in the family for some time afterward.

And now another such peaceful week had begun. One evening three or four days after they had visited Kobe, Fukuko said to her husband, seated across the supper table from her: "That movie the other day wasn't any good at all, was it?" She enjoyed drinking saké, and there was a little rosiness now around her eyes. "What did you think of it?" she continued, lifting the small bottle on the table. Shozo snatched it from her hands and poured for her.

"Here, have another."

"No, no, I can't . . . I'm drunk already."

"Oh, just one more. . . ."

"It never tastes as good, drinking at home. I have an idea—let's go somewhere tomorrow!"

"That'd be nice. . . . Yes, I'd really like to do that."

"I've hardly used any of my pocket money yet. After all, the other night we ate at home and then just went and saw that movie. So I've still got plenty."

"Well, where could we go?"

"I wonder what's playing at Takarazuka this month. . . ."

"A musical, I suppose." If they did go to the all-female revue at Takarazuka, Shozo could look forward to a good soak in the old hot spring there; but, even so, he didn't seem very keen on the idea.

"If you've got so much money left, couldn't we find some place more fun than that?"

"Well, think of some other place, then. . . ."

"What about going to see the autumn leaves?"

"At Minoo, you mean?"

"Minoo's no good—it was completely flooded last time. I was thinking it'd be nice to visit Arima. . . . It's been ages since we went. . . . What do you say?"

"Yes, when was it we were there?"

"Just about a year ago—no, wait a second. We heard those singing frogs, remember?"

"That's right. So it's been a year and a half now."

Their thoughts drifted back to the time just after their affair had begun. One day they had arranged to meet at Takimichi, the last station on the main line; they had then gone to Arima on the Kobe–Arima tram and spent a half-day amusing themselves in a room upstairs at the Gosho-no-bo inn. Both of them clearly remembered that pleasant summer day spent drinking beer and dozing as they listened to the cool sound of a mountain stream.

"Well, then, should we make it upstairs at the Gosho-no-bo again?"

"It'll be even nicer now than in the summer. We can see the autumn leaves, have a long, hot bath, take our time over supper—"

"Oh, yes—let's! Good, it's all settled!"

They had planned to have an early lunch the next day, but Fukuko didn't even start to get herself ready until around nine.

"God, your hair looks terrible," she said, looking at him in the mirror she was using.

"Probably. I haven't been able to go to the barber for over two weeks now."

"Then why don't you run over and get it cut? Be back in thirty minutes."

"That's impossible!"

"I don't want to be seen with you looking like that. Now hurry up and go."

Shozo ran to the barbershop, about half a block to the east of his own shop, with the one-yen bill his wife had given him fluttering in his left hand. Fortunately, there were no customers ahead of him, and he greeted the owner of the place, who emerged from a back room, with the words "Make it quick, please."

"Are you going somewhere?"

"To Arima, to see the autumn leaves."

"That'll be nice. . . . Your wife going too?"

"Yes. We're going to have an early lunch and leave right away, so she told me to get my hair cut and be back in thirty minutes."

Thirty minutes later Shozo left the shop, hardly hearing the barber's good wishes directed at his back: "Have a nice trip. Take your time, and enjoy it!" He arrived in front of his house and, happy as a clam, had just set foot inside the shop, when the ominous sound of his wife's voice from somewhere within froze him to the spot:

"And why did you hide this till today, Mother, may I ask?. . . Why didn't you tell me something like this had happened?. . . Have you just been pretending to be on my side, and really been letting him carry on like this the whole time?"

Shozo could tell that Fukuko was in quite a state by the peculiarly shrill tone in which all this was said. His mother had clearly been driven into a corner. She tried to defend herself with a word or two now and then, but she mumbled as if unsure of herself, and Shozo could hardly catch a thing she said. Fukuko's voice, however, resounded through the house.

"*What?*. . . It doesn't mean he went there? Don't make me laugh! He uses somebody else's kitchen to boil chicken in, and you say maybe it wasn't for Lily?! Where *do* you think he took it, for God's sake? And what about that paper lantern? You must have seen him bring it back and hide it away in there—you did, didn't you?"

It was most unusual for Fukuko to grab his mother and screech at her like this. The cause apparently was that, in the short time Shozo was at the barber's, someone from Kokusuido had come to collect the money and the old lantern he'd borrowed. After riding home that night with the lantern dangling on the front of his bicycle, he had, in fact, decided to hide it on a high shelf in the storage shed, so as to avoid any embarrassing questions from Fukuko. Unfortunately, his mother probably knew about it, and when the man from Kokusuido came by she must have gone to retrieve it. But why had he come for it, after saying that Shozo could return it any time? He couldn't care that much about an old paper lantern, surely. Maybe he just happened to have other business in the neighborhood. . . . Or was he angry because he hadn't got his twenty sen back yet? And was it the old man himself or a shop assistant? Whoever it was, Shozo couldn't see any reason for him to talk about the chicken business.

"If it was just the cat, I wouldn't say a word. Even if he says he's going to see Lily, it's *not* just Lily—that's what makes me so mad! And you, Mother—you think you can gang up with him to make a fool of me and get away with it?"

Faced with an attack like this, even O-rin was at a loss for words and had to pull back. It seemed unfair that his old mother should have to bear the brunt of Fukuko's temper when it was meant for him, and he felt sorry for her—but also just a little pleased: it served her right. At any rate, he was sure that if he'd been in the room with them, Fukuko would have gone berserk; and with the feeling of having barely escaped the tiger's maw, he got ready to rush outside as soon as danger threatened.

". . . No, I get the picture now! You *let* him go off to Rokko, and now you're making plans to drive *me* out."

These words were followed immediately by a great thud.

"Wait!"

"Take your hands off me!"

"But where are you going?"

"I'm going home. We'll see who's being unreasonable about this—"

"But Shozo'll be back any minute now—"

From the thumping and thudding, it seemed the two women were moving toward the front of the house as they struggled with one another. Shozo, panicking, shot out into the street and ran as fast as he could for five or six blocks. He couldn't have said what happened after that: before he knew it, he had reached the bus stop on the new national highway. He was still holding tightly in one hand the coins he'd received as change at the barbershop.

It was around 1:00 P.M. that same day. Shinako, a woolen shawl pulled on over her everyday kimono, had gone out by the back door at a brisk trot, saying she was going to deliver the sewing she'd done that morning to her customers in the neighborhood. Hatsuko was alone, working in the kitchen, when the paper screen slid open about a foot and a breathless Shozo stood peering into the room.

"Oh—" she cried, about to spring to her feet.

Shozo made a quick little bow, forced a smile, and said "Hatsu!" Lowering his voice and looking nervously behind him, he continued rapidly, "Shinako just left, didn't she?... I saw her back there, but she didn't notice me. I was hiding by those poplars over there."

"Was there something you wanted to see my sister about?"

"Certainly not! I came to see Lily." Now Shozo's voice changed, becoming charged with emotion, full of pain and sadness: "Hatsu, tell me, please, where is she? I'm sorry to bother you, but please let me see her, just for a few seconds!"

"Isn't she around the back somewhere?"

"That's what I thought, so I've been wandering around and standing under those trees for over two hours now. But I haven't seen a trace of her."

"Then maybe she's upstairs."

"Will Shinako be coming right back, do you think? Where did she go?"

"Just over there, to deliver some sewing. It's only two or three blocks away, so she won't be long."

"Oh God, what'll I do? What a mess!" Shozo shook himself violently and stamped his foot as he cried out. Then, rubbing his hands together as if in prayer, he said "Please, Hatsu, I'm begging you. . . . Look . . . it's the only favor I'll ever ask you. Just bring her to me—please!"

"What are you going to do if you *do* see her?"

"I'm not going to *do* anything. If I can just see that she's all right, that'll be enough."

"You wouldn't be thinking of taking her back with you, would you?"

"Would I do something like that?. . . If you'll just show her to me, I swear I'll never come and bother you again."

Hatsuko seemed amazed and gave Shozo a look that bored right through him. Then, without a word, she went upstairs and at once came halfway down again. Thrusting her head toward the kitchen, she announced: "She's up here."

"She is?"

"I can't pick her up, so you'd better come yourself."

"You think it'll be all right?"

"Yes, but be quick about it!"

"Of course. . . . Well, I'll go up then."

"Hurry!"

As Shozo went up the steep, narrow stairs, his heart began to pound. He was thrilled to be allowed at last to see his cat, but he wondered how much she had changed. He was grateful for the fact that she hadn't died by the roadside somewhere, or got lost and disappeared, but was here, safe in this house. He wondered, though, if she might have been ill-treated and was now just skin and bones. . . . Surely she wouldn't have forgotten him in the space of six weeks; but would she come to him immediately with a warm and loving look? Or would she perhaps run away from him out of shyness, as she had that other time?. . . When they were in Ashiya, and he came back after being away for two or three days, Lily would cling to him and lick him all over, as if to say she'd never let him leave her again. If she did that this time, it would be more than he could bear to have to shake her off. . . .

"Here she is—" The curtains were drawn, shutting out the bright afternoon light. Shinako, cautious as ever, must have closed them before she left. As a result, the room was vague with shadow. In the dimness Shozo could make out a charcoal brazier of Shigaraki ware and, beside it, his beloved Lily, seated on a pile of cushions, her front paws folded under her, her back rounded, her eyes drowsily half-closed. She was not as thin as he had feared, and the sheen of her coat showed that she'd been receiving excellent care. Other evidence that she was being well looked after was the two cushions obviously reserved for her; also, she seemed to have just finished her lunch, including a raw egg—the eggshell and a rice dish, which had been licked quite clean, were in a corner on some newspaper. Next to them was a litter-box, just like the one she had used in Ashiya. Shozo suddenly noticed the distinctive smell, which he'd forgotten over so many weeks. Before, it had permeated the pillars, walls, floors, and ceilings of his house; now, it filled this small room. Sadness welled up inside him, and he cried out "Lily!" in a strangled voice. The cat, seeming to notice his presence at last, opened two dull, listless eyes and cast an extremely unfriendly glance in Shozo's direction. Apart from that, there was no expression of emotion. Folding her forepaws still more deeply under her, and twitching the skin on her back and at the base of her ears as if she were cold, she closed her eyes again with a look that expressed the need for sleep, and sleep alone.

The weather that day was good, but the air was still piercingly cold, so Lily probably didn't relish the idea of leaving the charcoal brazier's side. Then, too, her stomach was full, which would make moving even more of a chore. Shozo well understood this cat's indolent nature and was used to her occasional unfriendliness, so he wasn't particularly surprised. But when he saw her listless eyes with masses of mucus collected in the corners and the way she crouched there, looking strangely dejected, he felt (was it only his imagination playing tricks?) that in the short time since they'd parted, Lily had aged tremendously— she had a doomed look. It was the look in her eyes that especially struck him. Though she usually seemed quite drowsy in circumstances like this, today was different: her eyes were like those of someone taken sick at the side of the road—all vitality gone, utterly exhausted.

"She doesn't remember you. She's just an animal, after all," said Hatsuko.

"Nonsense. She's pretending not to know me because there's someone else watching."

"I wonder. . . ."

"It's true. . . . That's why, sorry, but I'd like you to wait out here for a bit, and let me just close the door."

"Why? What are you going to do?"

"Nothing. I'm just going to, well, hold her on my lap for a while."

"But Shinako will be back any minute."

"Hatsu, would you watch the gate from that room there and let me know the moment you see her? Please. . . ."

Shozo put his hand on the door and even as he spoke was slipping into the room, leaving Hatsuko shut outside.

"Lily," he said, moving forward to sit opposite her.

At first the cat just blinked at him with a peevish look that seemed to say "Shut up! I'm having a nice afternoon nap." But as he wiped away the mucus from her eyes and took her on his lap and stroked her neck, she seemed to accept it all with quite good grace; and after a while she actually began to purr.

"How've you been, Lily? Are you feeling all right? Is she taking good care of you—hm?"

Shozo showered all sorts of loving words on her, hoping she would remember how they used to flirt with each other, and start to push against him with her head, or begin to lick his face. But Lily just continued to sit there with her eyes shut, purring, no matter what he said. As Shozo kept patiently stroking her back, he himself calmed down a bit and began to look around the room. Shinako's precise and fastidious nature showed itself in every detail. Thus, even if she was going to be out for only two or three minutes, she would carefully close the curtains, as she had now. Moreover, though the small four-and-a-half-mat room was filled with various objects—a dressing table, a chest of drawers, the things she needed for her needlework, and the cat's dishes and litter-box—there was no disorder: everything was in its place. If you looked inside the brazier where the iron was thrust, you saw that the ashes laid over the glowing coals were raked into careful lines. Even the enameled medicine pot on its tripod over the brazier gleamed as if it had just been polished.

But the strangest thing of all was those eggshells in Lily's dish. Shinako had to earn her own keep now, and it couldn't be easy. Yet, despite her poverty, she was making sure that Lily was well nourished. And look how much thicker Lily's cushions were than Shinako's own. How on earth had she come to take such good care of a cat she'd once detested?

Shozo realized now that his own character was to blame for driving his ex-wife out, and for causing this cat too a great deal of pain. And now, this very morning, he hadn't even been able to enter his own house and so had drifted over here. As he listened to the sound of Lily's purring, and was half choked by the smell of her litter-box, he was stirred by strong emotions. Yes, it was true—Shinako and Lily were both to be pitied. But wasn't *he* to be pitied even more? He, who had no home to call his own?

Just then, there was the sound of rapid footsteps.

"Shinako is right at the corner!" said Hatsuko, flinging open the door.

"Oh my God!"

"You can't go out the back. The front—go round to the front! I'll get your sandals for you. Now hurry, hurry!"

Shozo tumbled down the stairs and rushed to the front entrance. He scuffed into the sandals Hatsuko had flung onto the floor and scuttled out into the street. Just as he did so, he caught a glimpse of Shinako from behind as she turned to go in at the back door. They had just missed each other! As if pursued by something dreadful, he ran at full speed in the opposite direction.

THE LITTLE
KINGDOM

Kaijima Shokichi was transferred to a post at the primary school in M. City, G. Prefecture, about two years ago, when he was thirty-six. He was a true "child of Edo" (as the capital was once called), having been born in Asakusa's Shoten-cho area. From childhood he had enjoyed learning, a taste perhaps inherited from his father, who had been a specialist in Chinese studies during the days of the Tokugawa shogunate. It was this fondness for learning, however, that had made him fail in later life, as he now sadly recognized. No matter how unsuited he might be to making his way in the world, if only he hadn't insisted on trying to become a scholar—if instead he'd apprenticed himself at some shop and worked hard there—by now he might have become a respectable merchant of some kind. At the very least he would have been able to support his family comfortably. It had been a great mistake from the beginning, his attempt to become a scholar despite the fact that he came from a family so poor that there was no question of his going on to middle school. When he finished higher-level primary school in his mid-teens, his father urged him to find a place as an apprentice somewhere; but he refused, and instead entered the Teachers' Training College in Ochanomizu.

Immediately after graduating at the age of twenty, he became a teacher at the C. Primary School in his home area, with a salary of eighteen yen per month. Of course at the time he had no intention of remaining a primary-school teacher forever: he would support himself in this way for a while and continue to study hard on his own. He would work on his favorite historical subjects—on the history of Japan and China; and finally he would even become a Doctor of Letters! His ambitions were that high.

Kaijima's father, however, died when he was twenty-four, and shortly afterward he married; little by little his former drive and ambition were worn away. In the first place, he was very much in love with his wife. Up till then he had been so engrossed in his studies that he never even looked at a woman. Now, as he experienced more and more of the joys of married life, he gradually grew contented with his not very distinguished lot; without even being aware of it, he was becoming more like the mass of ordinary men. Meanwhile, children were born, his salary rose a little, and in the end he lost all his earlier determination to succeed and make a name for himself.

His eldest daughter was born at the time of his transfer to the H. Primary School in Shitaya Ward, where he made about twenty yen a month. Over the next fifteen years he continued to teach, being sent to various schools throughout Tokyo, from the S. School in Nihombashi to the T. School in Akasaka, and so on. He received promotions, and reached the grade of "licensed schoolmaster" with a monthly salary of forty-five yen; but his family's living expenses had increased at a far greater rate than his salary, with the result that he was getting poorer with every passing year. Two years after his eldest daughter, his first son was born. Then, one after another, there came a total of six children, until finally, seventeen years after he began his career as a teacher, he moved with his entire family to G. Prefecture, at which time his wife was pregnant with their seventh child.

Kaijima had been born and raised in Tokyo and had spent half his life there. If he now made the sudden decision to move to the provinces, it was because he could no longer cope with the pressures of daily life in the metropolis. His last position in Tokyo was at the F. Primary School in Kojimachi Ward, located on the exclusive high ground to the west of the Imperial Palace, where many of the nobility and high officials had their residences. Virtually all his pupils were well-bred children from middle-class families or above. So the sad, shabby sight of his own children, who were attending the same school, was distressing: no matter how poor he and his wife might be, he wanted at least to see his children neat and well dressed. "Daddy, buy me a dress like hers!" "I'd like a pretty ribbon!" "Buy me those shoes!" and in summer "Let's go somewhere cool!"—when they pestered him for things like this, he felt all the more oppressed by a sense of his own inadequacy as a parent. In addition, he was responsible for the care of his old widowed mother. Being honest, conscientious, and warmhearted, he worried constantly about these things and was overwhelmed with feelings of guilt toward the members of his family. Far better, then, to leave expensive Tokyo behind and lead a more relaxed life in a provincial town. By doing so, he hoped to be able to give his family some sense of security and peace. He chose M. City in G. Prefecture because it was his wife's hometown and there was someone who could help him find a new position there.

M. was a small city about seventy miles north of Tokyo with a population of some forty to fifty thousand, and was well known for the production of raw silk. It lay in one corner of the broad Kanto Plain, at a point where the flatlands met the foothills of the central mountain range and began to narrow and close in on themselves. The outskirts of the city on all four sides were given over to mulberry fields as far as the eye could see. On a clear day beneath bright blue skies Mt. H., famous for its hot springs, and Mt. A., with its huge, imposing mass, could be seen from every thoroughfare, towering beyond the rows of tiled roofs. In the town itself, the cool, blue waters of the T. River flowed swiftly through a man-made waterway. The main road, along which ran a tram for the I. hot spring, had a brighter and livelier aspect than that of most country towns. All in all, the city had great charm.

It was at the beginning of May that Kaijima and his defeated little family first came to M., and the city and its surroundings were at their most beautiful: it was a brilliantly sunny day. The Kaijimas, used to living for so long in a squalid back-alley tenement in Kanda's Sarugaku-cho, felt as if they had been delivered from the depths of some dark, fetid pit and brought out suddenly into the clear light of day. They sighed with pleasure. The children went every day to play on the lawns of the park where the castle had stood, or in the shade of the cherry trees growing thick along the riverbank, or at the edge of the pond in the A. Garden, where wisteria in full bloom hung heavily in great clusters. Kaijima, his wife, and his mother, now well into her sixties, felt a sense of sudden release; and apart from their yearly visit to Kaijima's father's grave, they had no need or desire to see Tokyo ever again.

The D. Primary School where he now taught was on the northern edge of the city, and behind the playground the fields of mulberry trees stretched into the distance. Gazing from the classroom window at the bright rural scene, struck by the distant beauty of Mt. A. enfolded in violet-gray mist, he taught his daily classes with a sense of exhilaration. When he arrived, he was assigned to teach the third-year boys' class; and he continued to have the same group through their fourth and into their fifth year, so his contact with them spanned three calendar years. There were no very well-bred, carefully dressed children of the sort he'd had at the F. School in Kojimachi; but M. was the prefectural capital, after all, and not a simple country town, so he did have some boys from fairly wealthy families, as well as a few who were unusually bright. There were also some naughty lads who were more tricky and unmanageable than any he had dealt with in Tokyo.

Two of the boys—the son of Mr. Suzuki, who owned a textile mill and was an officer in the G. Bank, and the son of Mr. Nakamura, the president of the S. Hydroelectric Power Company—were particularly bright, and one or the other of them was always at the top of the class during the years Kaijima was in charge of it. Among the "bad boys," the clear leader was Nishimura, whose father was a pharmacist. Then there was Arita, a doctor's son; he was the class crybaby, "Mama's little boy," whose parents spoiled him with fancy clothes and so on. But Kaijima had always liked children and by now had spent almost twenty years looking after them, so he was genuinely interested in all his pupils, in their variety of character and outlook; and he treated everyone with the same impartial kindness. Occasionally he meted out some quite severe physical punishments or gave them a real tongue-lashing. Nevertheless, he had a good reputation among the students themselves, his colleagues, and the parents because, with his many years' experience, he obviously knew a great deal about children. He was known to be an honest, sincere, and competent schoolmaster.

It was in the spring, two years after Kaijima had come to M. City. At the beginning of the school year in April, a new pupil joined the fifth-year class he was in charge of: his name was Numakura Shokichi. He was a stocky, heavyset boy with a dark complexion and a rather melancholy look in his eyes; round-shouldered, square-faced, and with traces of a scalp infection visible here and there on his very large, pointed head. His father had apparently drifted over from Tokyo to work at the textile mill that had recently been built in one section of the city. It was evident from his rather common-looking face and grimy clothes that he was not the child of wealthy parents. Kaijima felt intuitively at their first encounter that this boy would be badly behaved and poor at his studies; but when he actually had the chance to observe him in class, he found he wasn't so lacking in ability after all. Moreover, he seemed more docile than one would have thought—a calm, quiet, taciturn lad.

Then one day Kaijima was strolling around the grounds during noon recess watching the pupils hard at play (this was a habit of his, since he firmly believed that if you wanted to learn something about a child's potential, you should pay more attention to what he did on the playground than to his behavior in class). He discovered that his own class had divided into two groups and were playing at war. That in itself was not unusual, but he was struck by the way they were divided up. Of the fifty pupils, forty were in one group and only ten in the other. The first was led by Nishimura, the pharmacist's son, who directed his troops with great earnestness as he sat astride two boys who served as his horse. The leader of the second, much smaller group was, to Kaijima's surprise, Numakura Shokichi, the new boy. This usually quiet lad was on horseback too; and with loud shouts and eyes blazing he commanded his troops to attack, himself taking the lead in charging into the enemy's massed ranks.

Numakura had been at the school barely ten days—how, then, had he come to wield such power? His curiosity immediately aroused, Kaijima followed the battle with the greatest interest; and, as he watched, a boyish smile spread across his face. For, in no time, the larger force began to give way, breaking formation and finally fleeing wildly in all directions. It was true that the members of Numakura's small army were all extremely strong boys—playground heroes; but the sheer cowardice shown by their opponents was amazing. They seemed particularly afraid of Numakura himself: no sooner did he come charging at them on his horse than they wavered and collapsed, not daring to put up a real fight at all. In the end, even the opposing general, Nishimura, quailed under that baleful gaze, surrendered, and was taken prisoner. Yet the victor himself did not use any violence; he merely broke through the enemy lines repeatedly from several directions, shouting orders to his troops and invective at the other side: "Right—let's do it again! This time we'll do it with *seven* men. Seven'll be enough for us!" And, sending three of his soldiers over to the enemy side, he joined battle again; and again Nishimura's army was soundly beaten. The third time, the seven were reduced to five; even so, Numakura's little band prevailed after a fierce struggle.

From that day on, Kaijima began to pay special attention to this new boy. In the classroom, though, there was nothing to set him apart from any of the others. He did quite well, whether he was made to read aloud from a text or to do some calculation; and he never failed to do his homework. Since he was always bent silently over his desk, his eyebrows knit together in a rather discontented-looking frown, Kaijima found it impossible to guess what the boy's character was really like. At any rate, he didn't seem to be a troublemaker, the sort who makes fun of the teacher, incites his classmates to mischief, and generally spoils the atmosphere of the class. He may have been "the boss" of the class, but was clearly not the usual type.

One morning during the ethics lesson, Kaijima told them the story of Ninomiya Sontoku, the early nineteenth-century sage. Usually when he taught, he spoke quietly, in a relaxed, affectionate way; but when it came to the ethics lesson, his manner changed, becoming noticeably more serious. It was the first class of this particular day, and bright rays of sunlight streamed through the windows. Perhaps because the air in the room was so fresh, the boys' mood too seemed more alert and attentive.

"Today I'm going to talk about Master Ninomiya Sontoku, so I want you all to be quiet and listen carefully." Hearing him begin in this solemn way, the class became perfectly still, fixing their attention on him. Even talkative Nishimura, who was often rebuked for chatting with his neighbor, today gazed up intently at the teacher's face, his bright, intelligent-looking eyes only blinking now and then. For some time, only the voice of Kaijima addressing his pupils could be heard ringing out over the mulberry fields around the school, while in the classroom itself the fifty boys sat listening with close attention, not making a sound.

"... And what did Master Ninomiya say then? How did he suggest the Hattori family could restore their waning fortunes? His instructions to the entire Hattori clan could be summed up in the single word 'frugality'!"

Kaijima continued to speak with a more fluent and forceful eloquence than usual, until he heard the sound of someone muttering to his neighbor in one corner of the classroom which, up to that point, had been completely silent. His face hardened for a moment. Now, just when everyone was quiet and paying such good attention—and indeed all the boys today seemed unusually keen to listen—who was disturbing the class with this unwelcome chatter? Kaijima made a point of clearing his throat noisily before continuing his lecture, directing a brief glare toward the offending corner. There was silence for a minute or two, and then the low whispers started up again. The sound grated on his nerves like twinges from an aching tooth. Inwardly furious, he turned abruptly to look in its direction every time he heard the voice; but it would stop at once, so he couldn't tell who was responsible. However, the noise came from the right rear corner of the room, the area where Numakura had his desk; and the teacher became convinced that he was the culprit. If it had been someone else—and particularly if it had been a mischievous boy like Nishimura—Kaijima would have pounced on him and given him a good scolding. But somehow Numakura seemed hard to scold. He was—how should one put it?—a child, yet not a child; and bawling him out would seem both unkind and rather bad-mannered on the teacher's part. For one thing, he didn't really know the boy as yet—he still hadn't had a chance to talk with him in a friendly way, apart from asking and answering questions in class. So Kaijima decided to ignore the whole matter if possible: he would let him off this time—the boy wouldn't go on talking much longer. . . . But, on the contrary, the voice grew louder and louder until finally he could clearly see Numakura's lips moving.

"Someone's been blabbing away there in that corner—now, who is it?" Kaijima was unable to control himself any longer, and as he spoke he struck the top of his desk with his rattan pointer. "Numakura! It's you, isn't it? You're the one who's been talking!"

"No, sir, it wasn't me. . . ." He stood up without the slightest sign of fear and looked around at the boys sitting near him. "He's the one who was talking," he continued, suddenly pointing at a boy called Noda who was sitting next to him, on the left.

"Oh no. I saw *you* talking, and it wasn't with Noda. It was with Tsurusaki, there on your right. Why are you lying like this?"

Kaijima's face reddened with an anger he'd never felt in class before. Noda, whom Numakura was trying to blame for his own offense, was a good-natured, well-behaved student. When Numakura pointed at him, he blinked in astonishment for a moment, then fixed an anxious, pleading look on the other boy. At last, seeming to come to some sort of decision, he rose to his feet and, his face pale and his voice trembling, said, "Sir, it wasn't Mr. Numakura. I was the one who was talking."

Most of the other pupils turned to look at Noda with mocking glances, which made Kaijima even angrier. Noda hardly ever chattered in class. Almost certainly he was being falsely accused by Numakura, who was now swaggeringly sure of his position in the class. Suddenly presented with the dilemma, Noda must have decided he had to take the blame for "the boss." If he refused, he was sure to be bullied by Numakura later. If this was true, as Kaijima suspected, then Numakura was all the more contemptible. There could be no question of letting him off without a full investigation and proper punishment.

"I'm asking Numakura, not you. Everyone else should be *quiet!*" Kaijima brought his stick down on the desk again with a thwack. "Numakura! Why are you lying? I saw you talking, so you'd better tell the truth. Come on, own up—you know you're in the wrong. If you apologize for what you did, I won't give you a bad time. . . . But you're not only lying, you're even trying to blame somebody else for it. That's the worst thing you could do. If you don't change your ways now, young man, you won't amount to anything when you grow up!"

Numakura remained completely undaunted, glaring up at Kaijima with those gloomy eyes of his. His expression had the toughness, malevolence, and ferocity that one often finds in young delinquents.

"Why don't you answer? Do you understand what I just said?" Turning over the ethics textbook which lay open on the desk before him, Kaijima moved swiftly to Numakura's desk. He flexed the rattan rod with both hands, making it plain that he would use it if necessary before he'd finished with this boy. The others held their breath; the tension was palpable. A hush fell over the room, a silence quite different from before, like that preceding a sudden storm.

"What's wrong, Numakura? Why don't you say something? How can you be so stubborn, after all I've said?"

Just as the rod's tip seemed about to fly out and strike him on the cheek, the boy spoke:

"I'm not being stubborn." His low, husky voice carried a tone of calm resolve, and his thick black eyebrows were drawn together even more tightly than before. "It really was Noda who was talking, sir. I'm not lying."

"All right—get over here!" Kaijima grabbed the boy by the shoulder and began roughly dragging him forward with a grim look on his face. "Get over here and stay standing below the podium until I say you can move. If you say you're sorry for what you've done, I'm ready to forget it. But if you go on being pigheaded, you can stay there all night!"

"Excuse me, sir. . . ." Noda stood up again. Numakura seemed to give him a swift, sidelong glance as he did so. "Really, it wasn't Mr. Numakura. Please let me stand there instead of him."

"No, there's no point in punishing you. You and I can have a little talk about this later."

As the teacher started tugging at Numakura again, another pupil got up: "Sir. . . ." It was Nishimura, the naughtiest boy in the class. Instead of his usual cocky, back-street manner, there shone in his face a noble courage and resolution, like a retainer about to lay down his life for his lord. His expression was so grave that it hardly seemed possible he was only a boy of eleven or twelve.

"I'm not going to punish someone for things he hasn't done. I'm punishing Numakura because he's guilty. Now, those of you who aren't involved, keep quiet!"

Kaijima was furious. He couldn't understand why everyone was trying to cover up for Numakura, particularly if they were being bullied and intimidated by him; it only made it harder to explain.

"You—I'm telling you to move, so hurry up!"

"Sir." Yet another student rose to his feet. "If you're going to make Mr. Numakura stand there, let me stand with him." To the teacher's amazement, it was Nakamura, a gifted student and head of the class.

"What?" Kaijima was stunned, and found himself relaxing his grip on Numakura's shoulder.

"Sir, let me stand with him too!" One after the other, five or six pupils left their seats and moved forward to form a small group around the podium. Then came almost every student in the class, pressing forward and surrounding the teacher, all of them repeating "Me too, sir, me too!" There was no trace of malice in their attitude, no apparent desire to embarrass their teacher. Like Nishimura, they were just intent on offering themselves to save Numakura.

Angry and upset, and hardly knowing what he was doing, Kaijima was on the point of shouting at them: "All right—I'll make you *all* stand there then!" Had he been younger and less experienced, he surely would have in his present state. But, true to his reputation as a veteran teacher, he could not allow himself to lose control completely in front of these fifth graders. At the same time, he couldn't help feeling secretly astonished at the strange authority wielded by this new boy.

"Look," he said, with obvious frustration, "Numakura has done something wrong and I'm trying to deal with it. Why are you objecting like this? You're wrong, all of you!" Then, feeling there was no other way, he abandoned his attempt to punish the boy.

The matter seemed to have been settled with the teacher's final admonition to the class. Yet Kaijima could not put the Numakura affair out of his mind; it stayed with him as a problem to be studied and resolved. Fifth graders in primary school are, after all, innocents. At the age of eleven or twelve, children tend to run wild, ignoring their parents' advice and their teachers' orders. Yet the whole class now seemed to accept Numakura as their unquestioned leader, and to be willing to do whatever he said. Not only Nishimura, who had thrown his weight around as the class "boss" until Numakura's arrival, but even honor students like Nakamura and Suzuki took orders from him, whether out of fear or real devotion; and if he was found to be at fault in something, they volunteered to be punished in his place. Granted his great physical strength and courage, he was still just a snotty-nosed kid, the same age as his companions; yet his classmates were clearly far more impressed by the words "Mr. Numakura said such-and-such" than by the statement "Teacher said so-and-so." In his long years as a primary-school teacher, Kaijima had encountered some extremely willful children and even young delinquents who were almost unmanageable, but he had never come across anything like this Numakura business. How had he made himself so popular with the entire class? How did he manage to dominate so completely a group of fifty lively students? It was unprecedented, in any of the many schools with which Kaijima had been acquainted.

It was not necessarily a bad thing to have brought the whole class under one's control, to be able to order them about as one chose. If this was the result of Numakura's moral leadership and natural authority, there wouldn't be the slightest reason to rebuke him. Kaijima was only afraid that the boy might be some sort of evil prodigy, a truly wicked child who could not be dealt with by any of the usual methods. Perhaps even the best elements in the class were being forced into unwilling obedience. . . . Perhaps Numakura would use his power gradually to promote evil ways and vicious habits among the other pupils. . . . With that degree of power and influence, if he did set out to corrupt the class, it would be disastrous. Fortunately Kaijima's eldest son, Keitaro, was in the same class, and by asking some casual-sounding questions, the teacher was able to reassure himself that his misgivings were unnecessary.

In response to his father's questions, Keitaro first paused as if wondering whether he should say anything or not, and then gave a brief, hesitant reply: "Numakura's not a bad kid, Father. . . ."

"Are you sure—really? I'm not going to use what you say against him, so don't be afraid to tell the truth. What happened during the ethics lesson the other day? Numakura misbehaved, and then tried to blame it on Noda, didn't he?"

In answer to this, Keitaro gave the following explanation. It was of course a bad thing to do, but Numakura hadn't really meant to get anyone into trouble. He had merely been trying to test his followers (meaning everyone in the class) to see how loyal and devoted they actually were. And as a result of what happened, he was able to satisfy himself that each and every boy in the class was prepared to sacrifice himself for him; and that even the teacher could do nothing about it. Noda, who had been the first to take the blame that day in response to Numakura's directive, as well as Nishimura and Nakamura who had followed suit, later received official recognition from him for their meritorious service as "the most loyal members of the class."

This much, at least, was clear from Keitaro's account, if one read between the lines. Asked just when and how Numakura had acquired so much authority, however, he was unable to come up with any definite explanation; but it seemed that Numakura was a genuinely brave, bighearted, and chivalrous lad, and that these qualities had gradually made him their natural ruler. In terms of purely physical strength, he was not necessarily unbeatable—Nishimura would probably have won in a wrestling match between the two. But Numakura never bullied the weaker pupils as Nishimura often did; so if the two of them quarreled, most of the children would support the new boy. Also, though he might be weaker in wrestling, when it came to a real fight Numakura was exceptionally tough. He exuded an air of authority, a spirit of command, and whatever courage his opponent might possess was virtually swallowed up. Thus, though there was a struggle for power between him and Nishimura shortly after he came to the school, the latter soon had to concede defeat; and not only "concede"—he willingly became Numakura's obedient underling. There was a generous, friendly side to his character, too. As a result, even those who at first were hostile to him ended by gladly obeying his orders. Even Nakamura and Suzuki, the honor students, who never readily gave Nishimura their allegiance when he was "boss," now became the most loyal of Numakura's followers, flattering and humoring him to stay in his good graces. Until Numakura arrived, Keitaro had looked up to these two boys; now, however, they had begun to seem very ordinary. Their grades might be excellent, but put them alongside Numakura and they were like children thrust into the presence of an adult.

For these reasons, then, there was no longer any opposition to Numakura whatsoever; everyone happily submitted to him.

Once in a while he would issue an order that was clearly arbitrary or selfish, but for the most part his methods were fair. All he wanted was that his rule be firmly established; once that was done, he hardly ever abused his power. If one of his followers bullied a weaker pupil or did anything else mean-spirited, he applied severe sanctions. Boys like Arita were therefore gladdest of all that Numakura was now in control.

Having heard all this from Keitaro, Kaijima couldn't help feeling an even greater interest in Numakura. If what his son said was true, then the boy was certainly not a troublemaker: he might be "the boss" of the class, but he was an admirable one. There was a chance, in fact, that this working-class lad was destined for great things. Some might argue that it was wrong to let a boy turn his classmates into underlings and boss them around—that harm would come from letting him get away with such behavior. Yet, if the others were ready to obey him, surely there was no need to interfere; and even if the teacher did try to step in, how could he expect to be effective? No, it would be far better to praise Numakura—praise him for having a fine sense of justice and chivalry despite his age, and encourage him to win even more popularity at school. Kaijima would guide him into being an influence for good, to the benefit of the whole class.

With this in mind, the teacher summoned Numakura to his desk one day after class: "I didn't call you up here to give you a scolding. In fact, I'm really impressed—even an adult would find it hard to accomplish some of the things you're doing. To get every pupil in the class to obey you isn't an easy job, even for a teacher; but you're doing it. It's actually rather embarrassing!"

This warmhearted teacher was saying what he really felt. Here he was, with twenty years' experience in education, being outdone by just a boy when it came to controlling the class. And it wasn't only himself—he wondered if there was a primary-school teacher anywhere who could do as good a job as "Boss Numakura" did at influencing children and winning their obedience. "We pride ourselves on being 'educators,'" he thought to himself, "but shouldn't we feel ashamed, considering how much Numakura has accomplished? Our affection for our students and their respect for us don't begin to come up to his standard. There's a sincerity, a purity, in children which *we* can't match, and so we're cut off—unable to join them in their games as equals. We can learn a lot from Numakura—we need to *work* to be accepted as their 'pals,' not held in awe as 'teachers'...."

Aloud, he continued: "I'd like you to keep up the good work—punish the ones who misbehave and encourage the ones who're doing well, so the whole group can grow into fine, well-mannered young men. I'm asking for your help, Numakura. We can't have a class 'boss' who's a roughneck and leads the others into bad ways; but if you're willing to work like this to make the class better, you'll be a real help to me.... What about it—do you understand what I'm saying?"

The boy apparently found it hard to take in this unexpected speech and stood looking up at the teacher's gently smiling lips. Then after a few moments he seemed to grasp what Kaijima meant, and said with the brightest of smiles "I understand, sir. I'll do just as you say." He could hardly contain his joy and excitement.

Kaijima himself felt a certain elation as well. He really *did* know how to deal with boys. He was skillfully guiding Numakura, a lad who could become quite unmanageable if he wasn't handled properly. His long experience in this job was paying off. The thought made him feel good.

The next morning when he went to school, the teacher found

firm evidence that his "Numakura Control Plan" was already working even better than he'd expected, and his secret sense of elation grew. The evidence lay in the fact that from that day on the atmosphere in his classroom was completely, and uncannily, transformed. There was no need for him to admonish any of the pupils, for all the din and chatter had ceased. The children were as silent as the dead. There was not a cough; everyone seemed to be holding his breath. It was so strange that Kaijima glanced discreetly at Numakura and found that, from time to time, he took a small ledger from his pocket, looked all around the classroom, and marked down what appeared to be demerit points against any boy who wasn't sitting up properly at his desk. "Ah, yes!" thought the teacher, unable to repress a smile. The new class rules were enforced and observed more strictly with each passing day, and, judging from the expressions on the pupils' faces, all of them were praying fervently that there should be no slip on anyone's part.

"How is it that this class has become so well behaved lately? You're so nice and quiet, I'm really impressed. No, not just impressed—amazed!" One day, Kaijima put on a show of wide-eyed surprise for the benefit of his pupils. The children, who had been waiting for some such words of praise, gave a great shout of happy laughter when they heard their teacher's comment.

"When you're good like this, you make me feel proud of you. Even the teachers of the other classes have noticed—and the principal too! He often says that you're so quiet and conscientious you're a model for the rest of the school. So you should all be aware of what a fine reputation you have and do your best to keep it, not just for the time being but always. Be careful you don't just make a good start and then give up halfway along, all right?"

The children greeted this with another burst of cheerful laughter. Numakura, however, merely locked eyes with Mr. Kaijima and grinned.

Almost immediately after the birth of their seventh child, his wife's health began to suffer, and she sometimes had to take to her bed. In the summer of that year, she was at last diagnosed as having tuberculosis. It had only been for the first year or so after moving to M. City that life had seemed a bit easier for the family. The latest infant was always sick, and Mrs. Kaijima no longer had any milk with which to nurse it. Kaijima's mother's chronic asthma worsened with every year that passed, as did her temper. The family's circumstances seemed to become more and more difficult—and now the news of Mrs. Kaijima's illness had plunged them all into deeper misery.

Each month, a full week before the approach of the thirtieth, Kaijima would become anxious and depressed. When he thought back to their days in Tokyo, where, though poor, they had all been healthy and in good spirits, it seemed a better time for them than the present, at least. They had more children now, and prices had risen; so the family expenses were not a whit lower than they had been in Tokyo—and that was not including the cost of the various medicines they needed. Then too, when he was young, Kaijima could depend on getting some fairly large increases in salary in due course; now, however, there was nothing to look forward to.

"Yes, and didn't the fortune-teller say that you were moving in a bad direction when you left Tokyo for here? That there'd be no end of sickness in the family? I said at the time we should go somewhere else; but oh no, that was just silly superstition according to you. And now look—look what's become of us!"

As Kaijima sat there sighing, wondering what to do, his mother would pester him with peevish remarks like this. His wife pretended not to hear and, holding back her tears, said nothing.

One day toward the end of June, Kaijima returned home in the evening after a teachers' meeting at school to hear the sound of one of his children sobbing by the bedside of his wife, who had been lying ill with a fever for two or three days. "So, someone's been scolded again." Kaijima understood the situation at once as he stepped over the threshold, and the thought pained him. Recently there had been a tense, unsettled atmosphere in the house. His mother and his wife were constantly picking on the children, who for their part were fretful and difficult because they were given no pocket money at all.

"Why don't you answer when your grandmother asks you a question? Surely you haven't been stealing things, just because I can't give you any extra money?. . ."

It was his wife's voice, and her words were broken by hollow coughs. Amazed at what he heard, Kaijima threw open the door to the sickroom and found Keitaro being closely questioned by his mother and grandmother. Hemmed in on both sides, the boy looked stiff and uncomfortable.

"Keitaro! What have you done now? Didn't I tell you just the other day that you're not to give your mother any trouble when she's ill like this? You're the eldest, but you just *won't* understand, will you?"

Keitaro remained silent with his head bent; from time to time he released great drops of pent-up tears onto the tatami mats.

"For the last two weeks I've been noticing something strange about Keitaro's behavior. . . . And now look what sort of person he's turned into!" Kaijima's mother too had tears in her eyes and spoke in a choked voice as she gazed at her son.

Kaijima began to question Keitaro and soon discovered his mother had ample grounds for being angry. The boy should not have had even an extra penny left this month after buying the basic school supplies. Yet he was bringing home various things, sweets and so on, from somewhere or other. A little while ago his mother had noticed that he had five or six colored pencils and, thinking it odd, had asked him where he got them. From someone at school, he said. Then the day before yesterday he'd come home in the evening, hidden himself in a corner of the corridor, and begun stuffing something into his mouth. His grandmother sneaked up on him and discovered that his breast pocket was crammed with packets of sticky rice cakes. Come to think of it, Keitaro had stopped nagging his parents for spending money lately, which was unusual. And once the women's suspicions had been aroused in this way, they remembered several other worrying things. The whole situation was so odd that they had decided to look into matters a little more closely at the next opportunity. Then, today, Keitaro had come home with an elegant fan which must have cost at least fifty sen. This too was alleged to be "from a friend." But when asked who this friend was, and when and where he gave the fan to Keitaro, the boy just hung his head, refusing to reply. Becoming even more suspicious, they grilled him until at last they squeezed a confession out of him: it wasn't a gift but a purchase! Yet when asked just where he had got the money to buy something like this, he still refused to say, no matter how harsh they were with him. He only kept stubbornly insisting that he "hadn't stolen any money from anybody."

"If you didn't steal it, then where did it come from? Tell me that. . . . *Tell me!*" His grandmother became so furious that she

123

seemed to forget her own illness and to be on the point of hitting Keitaro.

Kaijima, listening to all this, felt a chill pass over him, as if he'd been doused with cold water.

"Keitaro, why don't you tell the truth? If you stole it, just come right out and say so. . . . You know I want you to have the sort of things any boy wants; but with things as they are, with so much sickness in the family, I just don't seem to be able to look after you the way I should. I know it's hard on you, but you just have to put up with it. I don't like to think you're the type of boy who'd steal someone else's property, but sometimes we all act on impulse—we don't intend to, but suddenly we find ourselves doing something rotten. If that's what happened, tell me the truth now, and I'll forgive you this one time. Tell the truth, apologize to your grandmother, and promise you'll never do it again. . . . Keitaro! Why don't you say something?"

". . . But Father, I . . . I *didn't* steal anybody's money. . . ." The boy began to cry again.

"But you say you bought all these things—this fan, and the colored pencils, and the sweets the other day. So where did the money come from? How can I believe you if you won't tell me that? I'm not going to stand for much more of this, young man. Be stubborn now and you'll regret it—you understand that, don't you, Keitaro?"

A great wail suddenly burst from the boy. His mouth worked convulsively, but for a time his blubbering made it impossible to catch what he was saying. At last, though, Kaijima realized that his son was offering excuses, awkwardly repeating the same thing over and over through his tears: "It's not *real* money—it's just fake stuff. . . ." The boy drew from his pocket a crumpled bill, holding it up and rubbing the tears from his cheeks with the back of his hand.

His father took the bill and spread it out on his lap. It was just play money for children, with the words "One Hundred Yen" printed in medium-sized type on a small slip of Western-style paper. It became clear that Keitaro had another four or five of them hidden away in his pocket: fifty yen, one thousand yen, even ten thousand yen—the larger the amount, the bigger the size of the type and the bill itself. And in one corner on the back of each bill was a personal seal that read "Numakura."

"This is Numakura's seal! Did he print these bills?"

Kaijima guessed the general nature of the situation and heaved an inward sigh of relief; still, he remained suspicious.

"Unh ... unh," said Keitaro, jerking his head up and down and crying even harder. At last, after a whole evening spent first in calming the boy and then in coaxing the story out of him, Kaijima was able to get to the bottom of the business about the play money. Numakura's power had, as he'd foreseen, continued to grow, and by now had resulted in an extraordinary, yet almost unnoticed, situation.

From what Keitaro revealed, it seemed that despite the apparent success of the "Numakura Control Plan" on which Kaijima had so prided himself, it had recently begun to produce several unwelcome side effects. Numakura, having received unexpected praise and encouragement from his teacher, became tremendously pleased with himself and began to act with even more than his usual self-confidence. First of all, he made up his own class-list and started keeping a detailed record of each boy's daily behavior, giving strict marks according to a system of his own devising. "Present ... Absent ... Tardy ... Left Early"—he recorded such things as a matter of course, with the air of authority of a regularly appointed teacher. In addition, absentee students were required to provide reasons for their absences; and secret investigators were dispatched to determine whether these excuses were in fact valid or not. Pupils could not get by with any old excuse: if they were late for class because they'd dawdled on the way, or had faked being sick in order to have the day off, the secret agents would be on to them at once.

Hearing this, it suddenly dawned on Kaijima that there had been no cases of absence or lateness at all recently. Even Hashimoto, the sickly son of a kitchenware dealer in the C. district, came to school every day. He looked pale and listless, and yet, to his teacher's amazement, he was always there. Everyone, in fact, had become very studious. Kaijima had been extremely pleased.

A total of seven or eight children had been appointed as investigators. They hung about near the houses of pupils who were known to be lazy, quietly tailed them when they went out, and generally kept them under the strictest observation. There was, of course, a range of punishments prepared for those who disobeyed orders. In theory everyone was subject to these penalties, including the head of the class and even Numakura himself.

As the variety of punishments gradually increased, the methods of applying them became more complex, and the number of investigators grew. In time, it became necessary to appoint various other types of officials. The class leader selected by Kaijima was simply set aside and in his place a strong, tough lad was made Inspector. Then there were the officials in charge of the attendance records, the playground, and recreation. A Special Assistant to President Numakura was appointed, as were a Magistrate and an Assistant Magistrate. There were also subordinates assigned to carry out the high officials' orders: Vice-President Nishimura, for example, being the second-in-command, had two aides working for him. And even the honor students, Nakamura and Suzuki, who at first were ruled out for being too weak, gradually won Numakura's respect and became Presidential Advisers.

Next Numakura devised a system of awards and honors. Lead medals were bought at a toy store, and the Presidential Advisers were instructed to supply appropriate designations for the various grades. Numakura then presented the medals to especially deserving followers. Soon there was yet another official, in charge of all these decorations. Then one day Vice-President Nishimura proposed that they appoint someone as Minister of Finance and begin issuing currency—a plan readily approved by the President himself.

Immediately they named a boy called Naito, the son of a liquor dealer, to this post. His duties for the moment consisted in shutting himself up on the second floor of his house with two assistants as soon as classes ended every day, and printing bills of various denominations ranging from fifty to one hundred thousand yen. The finished products were sent to the President to be stamped "Numakura," after which they became legal tender. All the pupils received a salary from the President, the amount depending on their rank: Numakura's own monthly salary was five million yen; the Vice-President's was two million; and the ministers each received one million, with their subordinates getting ten thousand yen.

The children soon began to use their newfound wealth to buy and sell things among themselves. Someone as rich as Numakura could buy whatever he liked from his followers. This meant that if, as often happened, the President decided to requisition one of the more expensive toys that a few of them possessed, it had to be handed over, however unwillingly. Nakamura, for example, whose father was head of the S. Hydroelectric Power Company, sold his Taisho zither to Numakura for two hundred thousand yen. The Arita boy had to give up the air rifle his father had just brought him from Tokyo—Numakura's offer of five hundred thousand yen was one he could not refuse.

At first these transactions were carried out in a random fashion in the school playground, but eventually they became large-scale operations: every day after school a market to which everyone came was set up in an open area of a park, or in a grassy place on the edge of town, or at Arita's house in the T. district. Finally Numakura made a law requiring anyone who received pocket money from his parents to buy goods with that money and bring them to the market. After that, the children were absolutely forbidden to use anything other than the bills issued by the President, the only exceptions being for small purchases of everyday necessities in local shops. Naturally under these circumstances boys from rich families were always forced to become sellers; but the buyers would in turn sell the goods to other children. Thus, gradually, the wealth of the citizens of the Numakura Republic became more equally distributed, and with access to the republic's currency even the poorest boys had money to spend. Though initially the transactions were done half in fun, the results were so good that by now everyone was full of praise for the President's enlightened rule.

Such, at least, was the picture Kaijima formed from the bits of information his son provided. Apparently a very broad range of items was bought and sold in the children's market; Keitaro himself listed over twenty kinds of things when questioned that evening—Western-style paper, notebooks, photograph albums, picture postcards, rolls of film, sweets, cakes, roast sweet potatoes, milk, soft drinks, all kinds of fruit, children's magazines, books of fairy tales, paints, colored pencils, toys, sandals, clogs, fans, medals, purses, knives, and fountain pens. Virtually all of the boys' needs and wants were met by this array of goods assembled at the market.

Keitaro, as the teacher's son, received special treatment from Numakura and was never short of money. Probably Numakura knew the difficult situation the family was in and generously decided to help him out. At any rate, the boy always had about a million yen in his pockets, which was roughly the same amount as one of the ministers might have. He'd been able to buy all sorts of things, in addition to the colored pencils, sweets, and fan that his grandmother had discovered and questioned him about.

Numakura, however, was worried that this currency system of his, if discovered, would draw down Mr. Kaijima's wrath, even if his other measures did not. And so he made the children promise never to show the bills in their teacher's presence, and to be very careful that he not somehow find out about the new system. A special regulation was devised, providing severe punishment for anyone who ratted. This put a particular strain on Keitaro, since he was the most likely suspect; and, sure enough, when accused tonight of being a thief, he had cracked and revealed everything. No wonder he'd been so stubborn, and wailed and cried: he was scared of the punishment that would be meted out tomorrow.

"Don't be such a coward. There's nothing to cry about. If Numakura gives you a hard time, I'll teach him a lesson he'll never forget. . . . But what a sorry bunch you all are! I'm going to give the whole class a good talking-to tomorrow. . . . Never mind, never mind—I'm not going to say you told on them."

As his father scolded on, Keitaro shook his head, as if he hadn't heard a word: "It's no good! Everybody's suspicious of me already. . . . There's probably an agent listening to us right now!" And again the boy burst into tears.

Kaijima sat there stunned for a few moments. What if he did call Numakura out and reprimand him first thing tomorrow— what then? How should he handle the whole affair? What should he do? He was so shocked and amazed that he was barely able to frame these questions to himself.

One day toward the end of autumn that year, Kaijima's wife coughed up a large amount of blood; she took to her bed, and it was obvious she would have to stay there quite a while. His mother's asthma too got worse and worse as the weather grew colder. The air in M. City was rather dry, perhaps because it was so close to the mountains, and this seemed to aggravate both illnesses considerably. The house had only three rooms, of eight, six, and four and a half mats' size; and the two women lay side by side on their quilts in one of them, coughing and spitting phlegm.

The eldest daughter, Hatsuko, who was a first-year middle-school student, by now was doing all of the cooking for the family. She would get up while it was still dark to light the kitchen stove, carry food trays to her sick mother and grandmother, and look after her brothers and sisters. After drying her hands, which were chapped and cracked with the cold, she set off for school. During the noon recess she came home again and spent what time she had preparing lunch. Then, in the afternoon, there was washing to be done and the baby's diapers to be changed. Her father couldn't bear to watch her doing all this by herself, so he tried to help by fetching water from the back and giving her a hand with the cleaning.

One might suppose that the family's misfortunes had reached

their peak, but in fact there was every sign that there was worse still to come. Kaijima began to fear that he too had caught tuberculosis. He even found himself hoping that, if this was so, the children would also become infected so that the whole family could die together, leaving no one behind. And, indeed, Keitaro had begun to have night sweats recently, and to cough in a peculiar way.

With all his mounting problems, Kaijima frequently lost his temper in the classroom nowadays. He became irritated over trifles; the slightest thing set his nerves on edge and sent the blood rushing to his head. At times like these he felt like breaking off the lesson and running outside somewhere. One day he caught one of the pupils with some of Numakura's bills in his hand. "You've *still* got those things, after what I told you?..." He found himself shouting at the child; his heart was beating wildly, darkness welled up around him, and he seemed on the verge of falling down.

The students, with Numakura in the lead, began to make fun of their teacher, doing spiteful things that they knew would upset him. Even his son was shunned: he lost all his friends, and after coming home from school would spend the rest of the day moping in the Kaijimas' cramped rooms.

It was a Sunday afternoon toward the end of November. Kaijima's wife had had a fever for two or three days and was lying in bed, thin and haggard-looking. Their baby lay in her arms. It had been fussing since around noon, but now it was getting more and more cross and had begun to scream.

"Don't cry.... There, there, don't cry.... Shhhh ... hush now." The mother murmured these words from time to time in a tired, listless way. But in the end she fell silent, as if she no longer remembered or cared, and only the baby's shrieking echoed through the house.

Kaijima, who sat facing his desk in the eight-mat room next door, felt an unpleasant tingling in his ears and a slight trembling of the paper sliding screens each time the baby shrieked. He felt as if something oppressive were wrapping itself around his waist and up across his back; waves of irritation coursed up his body, starting at his feet. But he endured these almost unbearable sensations in silence and didn't budge from his desk.

"Let it cry if it wants to. . . . All you can do is leave it be until it wants to stop." It seemed as if all of them—father, mother, grandmother—had come to the same despairing conclusion.

That morning, they'd discovered that there was not a drop of milk for the baby, instead of the two or three days' supply they thought they had. At the same time, a still more painful fact was brought home to them: until Kaijima got his salary two days later, they wouldn't have a penny in the house. Each of them was afraid to speak of it, and tried silently to read the others' minds. As always at times like this, Hatsuko prepared some sugared water and cooked a bit of rice gruel, but the baby for some reason would not touch any of it. "Mma-mma, Mma-mma," it said, and burst into louder, angrier screams than ever.

As he listened to the baby's voice, Kaijima seemed to move beyond sorrow into some broad open place where there was neither pleasure nor pain. If it wanted to cry, let it cry as hard as it could. "Harder—cry harder!" He heard the words deep inside himself. Then, in the next instant, his nerves began to tingle with tension and his body seemed to be lifted into the air. He was aware of himself only from the shoulders up. After a while, he rose abruptly from his desk and began to pace fretfully back and forth.

"All right. I don't have to be afraid to ask just because there are a few unpaid bills. . . . His son is one of my pupils, after all. If I say I want to put it on my bill, he'll say 'Any time'll do—whenever it's convenient, sir.' There's nothing to be ashamed of. I'm just too timid, that's all. . . ."

His head full of such thoughts, he walked round and round a single spot in the small room, going over the same things endlessly in his mind.

Around dusk he wandered outdoors and started off in the direction of the Naito Liquor Store in the K. district. As he came up to it, a clerk who was standing in front of the shop bowed his head in greeting. Kaijima stopped for a moment in the road and, smiling, returned the bow. Behind the store counter, in one corner of a shelf packed with canned goods and bottles of liquor, he caught sight of two or three cans of milk. But Kaijima walked on, as if he hadn't noticed.

On the way back, nearing his house, he realized the baby was still crying. Its ear-splitting howls carried ten yards or more through the quiet twilight. Giving a start, Kaijima turned back again and began walking without any idea of where he was going.

The winds from Mt. A., which was one of the best-known features of the city, blew along the streets in cold blasts that warned of the winter soon to come. Beneath the embankment of a park that faced the river, five or six boys sat crouched in the darkness, playing some game or other; whatever it was, it involved a great deal of earnest whispering.

"Oh no, Naito, that's no good. You're trying to cheat me. I've only got three left, so I'll sell you one for a hundred yen."

"That's too much."

"Too much? You're crazy! Right, Mr. Numakura?"

"Yeah. Naito's trying to pull a fast one. You said you didn't

133

want to sell 'em, but he insists, and then tries to beat the price down. If you want to buy, pay the price, Naito."

When he heard this last voice, Kaijima stopped in his tracks and turned to look at them.

"Hey, what are you kids doing?"

The boys were about to make a run for it, ready to scatter in all directions; but Kaijima was too close—they never would have made it.

"So he's got us, and he's gonna give us a lecture—okay, big deal." Numakura's attitude was plainly written on his face.

"How about it, Numakura—how about letting me join your little group? What've you got for sale at your market? Give me some money and I'll join the game."

Kaijima had a broad smile on his lips as he spoke, but his eyes were strangely bloodshot. The children had never seen such a look on their teacher's face before.

"Okay, let's get started. No need for you guys to hold back— from today on, Teacher's going to be Mr. Numakura's man! I'm taking orders from him now, just like the rest of you. So you see, there's nothing to be shy about. . . ."

Numakura staggered back a few steps, his eyes round with surprise. But he recovered quickly, went up to Kaijima, and with the cool assurance of a playground "boss" addressing one of his young underlings said, "You mean that? Okay—I'll give you some of this money here. . . . There you go, one million yen." He took that amount from his wallet and handed it to Kaijima.

"Hey, this is fun! Teacher's gonna join our group!" shouted one of the children standing there, and several others clapped their hands excitedly.

"Teacher, Teacher, what can we do for you? Just tell us what you want!"

"Cigareeettes . . . maaatches . . . beeer . . . sakéee . . . soft driiinks. . . ." Someone shouted out the names of various goods, imitating the vendors in the kiosks at tram stops.

"Me? I'd like a can of milk—do you sell that in your market?"

"Milk? We've got some in the store at home—I'll bring it to the market tomorrow for you. And you can have it for just a thousand yen, since you're our teacher." It was Naito, the son of the liquor store owner, who was speaking.

"Okay, fine. A thousand yen's cheap. . . .* Well, I'll be back tomorrow, so don't forget the milk. . . ."

"Got it!" Kaijima thought to himself as he moved away. "Tricked 'em into selling me some milk. Good work! I really *am* pretty good at dealing with children. . . ."

On his way home from the park, Kaijima passed in front of the Naito Liquor Store. Suddenly, he went inside and asked for a can of milk.

"Let me see. . . . The price was, uh, a thousand yen, wasn't it? Here you are—I'll put it right here." No sooner had he taken out one of Numakura's bills than he gave a start and blinked, as if waking from an awful dream. His face turned red.

"My God, I must be crazy!" he told himself. "Anyway, I caught it in time, thank heavens. But what a stupid thing to say! I don't want people thinking I've gone mad—I'll have to think of something. . . ."

Kaijima gave a loud laugh and spoke to the shop clerk: "Just a joke, of course, pretending it's real money. But keep it anyway. On the thirtieth, you can give me back this chit, and I'll give you the thousand yen in cash. . . ."

---

*A thousand yen in real money was approximately a cabinet minister's annual salary at the time.

PROFESSOR
RADO

I

It would be the first time for the reporter from the A. *Journal* to meet Professor Rado, and it was with considerable curiosity that he had been waiting for something over an hour. There was still no sign of his host. The student houseboy who had let him in had announced "I'm afraid the professor is not awake yet. . . ." The reporter had heard that he slept late in the morning, and had planned his visit accordingly. But it was twelve-thirty by now! How could anyone sleep till past noon at the end of March, when the early cherries were already about to bloom? Feeling rather hungry as he thought about the professor and his habits, he gazed through the glass doors of the sitting room into the garden, bright in the noon sunshine.

It was not a very big garden for a house in the suburbs of Tokyo, but it was quite well cared for. The path leading from the low front gate with its brick pillars to the front porch was lined on both sides with carefully planted azalea bushes, and beyond there was a lawn. There was also a rectangular flower bed, bordered with tiles. Perhaps Professor Rado, bachelor that he was, did a little gardening with the help of his houseboy and maid? But it was not only the garden that was well looked after: the room where the journalist now sat was extremely neat, clean, and pleasant. In the course of his work, he had seen a great many reception rooms, in the homes of scholars, politicians, and businessmen; but the professor had clearly profited from his long stay in the West—the way the pictures were hung

and the furniture was placed, the color scheme of walls and curtains, all had been carefully thought out. It was a simple, cozy
room, but also smart somehow; it had been cleaned till there
was not a speck of dust, and the chair covers and tablecloth were
pure white, as if they'd only just been laundered. From all this,
it seemed safe to assume that the professor was a fastidious person—or was it the way of middle-aged bachelors to be rather
fussy about such things?

The gentleman from the A. *Journal* had not come to ask the
professor about anything in particular—that is, he was there
only to gather material for a series called "Visits with Eminent
Figures in the Academic World" which was appearing in every
issue. So it had not been altogether a waste of effort for him to
gather information about the professor's interests before their
meeting, especially since the reporter knew his subject to be a
difficult man, an egotist who rarely gave a kind reception to jour-
nalists who came to interview him. When in a bad mood, he
would barely speak a word, apparently; so the reporter had made
the journalistic judgment that he should begin by talking about
the professor's personal interests. He had lit his third Shikishima
cigarette and, having surveyed the garden, had begun to take
another careful look around the room when he heard a creaking
sound from the corridor, and an old man's heavy footsteps.
Then there was the sound of someone clearing his throat—
"Ahhemm, ahhemm"—and at last Professor Rado entered.

"Ah, this is a difficult man all right, just like they said." The
thought flashed through his mind as he swiftly put his half-
smoked cigarette in an ashtray, rose from his chair, and expressed his respect for the professor with a deep, stiff, military-
style bow. The latter was a man of about forty-five or -six, or
perhaps forty-three or -four. With his hair carefully parted over
a pyramid-shaped head, he didn't really look his age, if one

ignored the two or three white hairs that appeared at his temples. His face, however, was not so much fleshy as swollen, with an unhealthy pallor to it; and this gave him a sullen, angry look. His eyelids too were puffy, which made him seem even more severe. Whether because he had just woken up, or because he really was unwell, his face had the unpleasant color of someone suffering from a kidney disease.

"Sorry to have kept you waiting."

"Not at all. . . . Please forgive *me* for disturbing your rest."

The professor took a seat, so the journalist also allowed himself to sit down, slowly and reverentially.

"This is a very nice, quiet neighborhood, isn't it? Have you been living here for a long time, sir?"

"Long? Mmm. . . . Not really. . . ."

"About how many years? Two or three?. . . Three or four, perhaps?"

"Yes, well. . . ." And here the conversation broke off. No matter how politely and humbly the reporter put his questions, the professor gave only vague half-answers. In addition, his voice was extremely low, with a nervous tremor to it, and he swallowed the ends of his words. He had the reputation of being an arrogant man; but with his habit of looking away from the person he was speaking to, and quickly averting his eyes if they happened to meet the other person's, there was a certain girlish timidity or even cowardice in his manner.

The reporter resigned himself to saying nothing for a while and concentrated instead on a careful observation of his clothes. Having seen the house, he had expected its owner to appear properly dressed, in keeping with the appearance of the garden and sitting room; how amazed he was, then, at the professor's garb, which seemed to him strange to the point of weirdness. That odd-looking baggy garment, for example, like something a court judge, or a post-office clerk, might wear—what was it? From the waist up, it looked like a Russian peasant's blouse or some sort of Chinese coat, but the cut of the collar and the sleeves with drawstrings attached were different from either. It might have been the sort of dressing gown that Westerners wear over their pajamas, except for those drawstrings. The material was certainly a very thin, light silk weave, unusual stuff, not of Japanese manufacture; but it must have seen many years of use, to judge from its grimy sheen—it was so filthy that even the pattern was indiscernible. The collar was open, revealing a flannel undershirt and yukata beneath. The professor was still in his nightwear, then, and had probably put the baggy overgarment on to cover the fact. He may have felt that it didn't matter with just a second-rate journalist; but, in any event, this lazy, sloppy look was oddly out of place in the clean and orderly atmosphere of the room itself. Nor did it do the wearer much credit. He could at least have kept his collar decently closed; instead, it gaped wide, giving a clear view from his neck down to his chest. The reporter found it hard to admire this sort of seediness.

Looking at the professor's chest, his guest also noticed how fat he was in general. This fatness, though, was either a kind of swelling, as with his face, or else sheer flab—it did not appear to be a healthy stoutness. Also, he noticed how from time to time the professor gave a belch smelling strongly of *miso* bean soup. For someone who, he knew, had traveled in the West, this seemed surprisingly bad-mannered, but presumably he was still feeling full after a hasty late breakfast. "Ahhh.... I bet it's not his kidneys but his stomach that's giving him trouble," thought the reporter. And, comparing his own belly's emptiness with the other's bloated state, he felt at once envious and disgusted.

"Er, Professor, I see you have a flower bed over there in your garden...."

"Yes." As he spoke, he flicked a covert glance at the journalist's face, then directed his gaze off into the distance—presumably looking at the bed in question. The light streamed in from the garden, casting a ray of spring sunshine even onto the professor's ashen face.

"The weather's got quite warm, hasn't it? It should be just right for gardening soon. . . ."

There was no response, so the reporter was forced to add another word or two:

"What sort of flowers, mainly, do you have in your garden, Professor?"

"Oh, nothing special. . . ."

"And do you do the planting yourself?"

"Uhh . . . well. . . ."

"I see." He didn't, of course, but he convinced himself he did.

"Perhaps we could talk a bit more about this particular subject—about flowers, and gardening. . . ."

"Unnh. . . . Except I really don't have much interest in that kind of thing. . . ."

"Yes, but, for example, what sort of flowers do you like, or dislike, or—"

"I like most flowers, I suppose. . . . That's about it." The professor gave another belch, swallowing it down along with the end of his sentence.

What a weird character he was! The reporter had met some difficult people in his line of work, but never anyone as odd as this. He sat staring into the professor's face with an amazed expression on his own, as if confronted with some rare sort of animal. The subject appeared not to mind in the least being stared at, and simply turned aside, ignoring his visitor. "Talking is too much trouble, but you can look as much as you like," he seemed to be saying. Did this man have any normal feelings or reactions whatsoever? Everybody makes a show of smiling politely when they meet others socially, but not this person. And even his unfriendliness was different from the usual kind: his occasional attempts to smile seemed to vanish as soon as they began. A sort of twitching would sometimes start around his mouth, and this spasm was the only indication that he'd been trying at all. He appeared to be pulled in two directions at once: "Perhaps it's wrong of me not to smile—but I don't feel like it!"

Moreover, whatever questions he was asked, he maintained the same bored, listless expression. He looked as if he were hoping the reporter would stop this stupid interview and hurry up and leave. Yet he never came right out and said "Go home"; he only gave the occasional loud sigh, clearly intended to be heard. He was like a timid person who has fallen into the clutches of an insurance salesman: prepared to go on for a couple of days if necessary, patiently repeating his noncommittal replies until at last the salesman gives up and leaves.

"Excuse me, but may I ask you a little about your daily life then, Professor? For example, what time you get up in the morning, what time you go to bed, when you usually do your research. . . . A few words on this subject, if you wouldn't mind."

The reporter had grown a bit bolder and, sure that the professor could find no excuse for not answering this type of question, he took from his pocket a notebook and Eversharp pencil.

"Well, what about it, sir? I *am* sorry for disturbing you like this when you're so busy, but—"

"I'm not particularly busy."

"Oh, really?. . . Well, then, you generally get up around what time? I've heard that you're not an early riser. . . ."

"I get up late."

"I see. . . . About what time? Eleven? Twelve?"

"Unnh."

"I see. . . . Thank you." The reporter scribbled something in his notebook.

"Presumably you stay up fairly late at night."

"I go to bed late."

"I see. . . . About what time?"

"Around three."

"Really, around three?. . . But on days when you go to the university, I suppose you have to get up somewhat earlier?"

"Uhh. . . . Oh well . . . not really."

"In that case, are all of your lectures in the afternoon?. . . Oh, I see, they *are*. . . . And how many times a week do you go in to teach, Professor?"

"Twice."

"I see. . . . And what days would those be, please?. . . Wednesday and Friday. . . . And on the other days, what sort of things do you do mostly? I suppose you must spend most of your time reading in your study. . . ."

"Unnh. Well, things like that. . . ."

"And what *kind* of books do you usually read?. . . Almost entirely specialized works, on philosophy?"

"Uhh. . . . Yes, well. . . ."

The reporter, who had been doing little more than beating the air about him, led on by the professor's "Uhh's" and "Yes, well's," now recalled something important and rushed to put his question:

"Oh, yes! There's a rumor that you might be leaving the university quite soon, sir. Is that the case?"

"Unnh, possibly. . . ."

"For what reason?. . . Would it be some dissatisfaction on your part with the university itself?. . ."

145

"Well, you know. . . . Going there's pointless."

"So you're going to devote all your time and effort to your own writing, is that it?"

"Well, if I feel like it. . . . Maybe I'll write for some magazine or something. . . ."

"I see." Having come to a dead end again, the reporter cast around for some other topic, twisting his shoulders as though trying to wriggle out of a pit he'd fallen into.

"Errr . . . forgive me for asking a question like this out of the blue, but your daily life, Professor—spending your days shut up in your study with your books, quiet, solitary—you know, the life of a bachelor scholar—I'd really like to hear your views on this whole way of life. . . ."

Knowing the professor would not give an immediate, fluent response to this question, the reporter plunged on:

"I suppose it's better really not to have all the cares of family life when you're engaged in intellectual activities, isn't it?"

"Unnh, it is."

"On the other hand, don't you sometimes feel a bit lonely living like this?"

"I've got used to it."

"So, then, you would say that the single life is less complicated, more congenial?"

"Unnh . . . less complicated. . . ."

". . . And more congenial?"

"Unnh."

"Yes indeed, I see. . . . Still, you must have the occasional visitor—students, or friends?"

"Hardly ever."

"Oh, really? Your house, now—it's, what shall I say?—it looks very well kept. Who, if I may ask, does all the cleaning, and . . . ?"

"The houseboy."

"Oh, the houseboy does the cleaning? And how many maids do you have?"

"Two."

"So you have one houseboy, and two maids, and then there's yourself of course—so there're four people living here?. . ."

"That's right—four."

"And of course that would be all you'd need, living by yourself, as you do. . . . Frankly, seeing your house like this, even someone like myself can understand why you feel that it's less complicated, and more congenial, to live this way. . . ."

". . . . ."

This time the professor didn't bother to reply at all. And when the reporter heard what he thought to be a sigh, and looked carefully, he saw that the professor's nostrils were open a little wider than before. He was yawning.

Was this an indirect way of telling him to leave? The reporter himself was getting quite hungry and had a good mind to withdraw at this point, even without any urging from his host. All the same, being only human, he couldn't help resenting the brusque reception he'd been given, and showing some stubbornness in return. Wasn't a little obstructionism called for? He'd like to prolong this rubbery dialogue for another twenty or thirty minutes, if he could. And so he decided to take his time about concluding the conversation. The professor, having finished yawning, was looking toward the flower bed again, with the same bored expression. The light from outside fell strongly on his face, making him narrow his eyes. The petulant, self-satisfied look this gave him reminded the other man of a cat basking in the sun.

"As I recall, the recent crackdown on radical ideology has caused a number of problems for people in political and academic circles. Now, what are *your* views on the matter, sir?"

147

"Uhh . . . uhh." From then on, no matter what he was asked, the professor simply gave a sort of groan. From radical thought to methods of preventing the dissemination of Russian propaganda; from universal suffrage to the relation between democracy and government by philosophers; and finally even to the Ministry of Education's proposals on orthographic reform and the use of romanization in writing the national language—the journalist brought up all of these topics, only to have each of them in turn dismissed with the same noncommittal "uhh's" and "aah's." It was like trying to wrestle with oneself.

A few minutes later, the reporter took his leave; but, still feeling resentful and also knowing that he didn't really have enough material for an article yet, he walked around the low wall surrounding the grounds after he'd passed through the front gate. He wanted to take another close look at the layout of the house, from the outside this time. It was a fairly new Western-style building, with gray painted walls; a single-storied structure, it seemed just the right size for four people. The reporter followed the wall to the rear of the house, which faced a hillock overgrown with shrubs and small trees; here the wall gave way to a sparse hedge of Chinese hawthorn, through which the garden and house could be seen quite well. That room over there, with smoke coming from its chimney—that must be the professor's study. And indeed it was like him to have chosen such a room, facing north, with little sunlight, and therefore gloomy.

In the midst of these reflections, the reporter heard a clanking sound, like a pump bringing water up from a well. Surprised, he looked in the direction the sound was coming from and saw a girl of fifteen or sixteen crouched by the edge of the well, still wearing her cotton nightie and busily brushing her teeth. After she had finished, she filled a metal basin with water and gave her face a perfunctory wash with the help of a hand towel. Then, instead of going to the kitchen, she walked briskly toward a door at the back of the house which opened onto the garden. Slipping off her worn-down wooden clogs with their bright red thongs and leaving them on the topmost of the stone steps leading up to the door, she disappeared into what he took to be the study.

The reporter had only had a glimpse of her as she passed in front of the hedge through which he was peering, so he couldn't say for sure; but it seemed to him strange that a maid should be just getting up and brushing her teeth at this hour. Besides, with the kitchen entrance on the other side of the house, surely it was a bit odd for her to be going into that room, and in her nightie! So what *was* she, then? One of the "two maids" the professor had mentioned? A young parlormaid? Yes, well, to some extent she did look like one; yet there was something in the way she carried herself, a certain nonchalance, that had little of the servant about it. Her complexion was a bit pallid. So was she perhaps the professor's "little something"? But surely she was too much of a child for that—a mere fifteen or sixteen. . . .

At any rate, the reporter's curiosity was not of the type to be so easily satisfied. Fortunately there was no one in the back garden, so he slipped through the small wooden gate set into the hedge and, hiding himself in the shade of some large *yatsude* plants that happened to be growing there, he crept to a point directly beneath the window of the room in question. Carefully craning his neck, he could see that the two curtains did not quite meet at the center of the window, leaving a small gap for him to peek through. Putting one eye to this opening, he saw that the room was in fact the study. In one corner was a stove with coals giving off a warm red glow. Along the walls were bookcases reaching to the ceiling, packed full of books. The center of the room was dominated by a huge desk like a butcher's chopping block; and on it lay Professor Rado, face down, with that peculiar coat of his rolled up to his waist, exposing the flannel pajamas he was wearing underneath. And as for the young girl, she was sitting on the professor's back, with both legs dangling down from the desk. Occasionally she gave his head a sharp little rap, or squeezed his cheeks hard, or shoved her fingers into his mouth. She didn't seem to be just playing, though. The expression she wore was a very serious, even gloomy one: she seemed to be carrying out some sort of duty she'd been assigned. Her face—and her hands and feet as well—were pale and delicate. Professor Rado's face was the same nondescript, ashen color as before, in the sitting room; and though he was letting the girl pinch and prod his puffy cheeks as much as she liked, he looked very bored.

Soon the girl, still sitting on top of him, picked up a little rattan cane and sent several strokes swishing through the air onto his fat buttocks, while firmly gripping him by the hair with her other hand. It was then, for the first time, that a somewhat livelier look came into the professor's eyes, and he let out a kind of moan.

The reporter peered at this scene for a good half hour, until, in a rather curious frame of mind, he made his silent escape from the back garden.

II

There is a rumor going around that Professor Rado has recently taken a wife. There's no guarantee that it is true; but it would not be unlike him to marry on the sly, without telling anyone, and act as if nothing had happened. At any rate, no one really knows the truth about it; but the word is that, by some strange twist of fate, the reporter from the A. *Journal* is involved in it all. And, in point of fact, he was the original source of the rumor.

Ever since his rubbery dialogue with the professor, the journalist had been too daunted to attempt another interview. He knew only that shortly after his visit the professor had resigned from the university, a fact he learned from the pages of the newspaper. "Oh yes, he was saying he'd like to quit teaching and concentrate on writing; so now he's retired," he thought to himself at the time. It was only out of casual interest that he wondered what kind of writing the man had been engaged in since their last meeting, or what sort of research he might be pursuing currently; but he supposed he was publishing articles in some academic journal or other. After several years the reporter too changed jobs, moving from the A. *Journal* to the B. *News*, where he was in charge of articles on the performing arts.

Then, at eight or nine one evening in March of last year, this arts-page reporter—as he now was—happened to be in Asakusa Park and decided to take a look at the Muyusai variety troupe which was performing just then at the Showa Theater. He didn't really care for this type of show; but the troupe included several former singers from the old days of musical revues, and there were two or three whom he'd been on close terms with. It was to see these old familiar faces, then, that he went into the theater. After visiting the dressing room, he was standing in the wings watching the show for a few minutes when he saw something very strange and unexpected.

"That's odd—Professor Rado, in a place like this?" At first he thought it must be a mistake. In the interval between different acts, some sort of ballet turn was being performed on stage by five or six young actresses. From the wings, the reporter could see a confusion of naked legs lifting and kicking, and beyond them, in a seat at the very front, the face of one spectator in particular. The more the reporter looked at him, the more he seemed to be, in fact, Professor Rado. Of course it was hard to tell for sure because of the line of footlights that blazed between the stage and the man's face; but that half-open mouth with its row of white teeth and the little smirk that contracted his features as he watched the show were exactly like the weird attempts at a smile he'd seen the professor make that afternoon some years before. From where he stood, the reporter could not get a clear view of anything from the neck down. Only that face emerged above the stage's level horizon, like a severed head set there for viewing. The professor's face had, surely, been sallow and swollen, whereas this one was a ruddy color—in that respect, they seemed different; but it may just have been due to the reflection from the footlights. As the reporter considered these possibilities, the footlights went out and colored ones came on—red, blue, green, purple. Professor Rado's head changed colors too—from red to blue to green to purple. It was quite a sight.

In any case, the whole thing was certainly very odd. No matter how eccentric he was, it was hard to credit that he would

152

actually come to Asakusa Park at such an hour to see a variety show. This misanthropic bachelor scholar who ought to be holed up in his gloomy, north-facing study—if it really was him, he must have some special motive for being here. The reporter from the B. News, full of the curiosity that went with his calling, moved from backstage around to the front of the theater and peered in at the audience from the corridor. He could see that the small auditorium had cheap seats in the center of the first floor and superior, Western-style seats a level higher on either side.

The man in question was sitting at the very front of the more expensive section, virtually alongside the orchestra pit. Presumably this was the best place for observing any slips made by the performers, and also for enjoying a view of the dancers' legs. At the same time, anyone sitting there had to accept the fact that he too could be easily observed from other parts of the hall—just as was the case with the special boxes for distinguished guests at the old Imperial Theater. That evening in particular, the better seats were quite empty, and as one looked across at them, there was only this solitary figure, like a lone island in an empty sea. He was wearing an inverness and a hunting cap; and now, during the intermission, he had pulled down the brim of his cap and inclined his head so that his face was half hidden by the collar of his coat. Clearly he didn't feel comfortable here. The reporter slipped into a seat behind him and from there peered beneath the cap's visor.

"Is that you, Professor? I hope you've forgiven me for intruding that time some years back. . . ."

Actually, he was not yet completely sure this was the man. But neither was he certain that, even if it *was* the professor, he would come out and admit his identity; and so he addressed him suddenly like this, hoping to draw him out.

"Uhh. . . ." The man shrank back a little, as if startled, then looked over his shoulder, glaring at his questioner. From that "uhh" alone, the reporter knew it had to be the professor. It was this ambiguous response, somewhere between a normal reply and a belch, that had so frustrated the reporter before. There could hardly be another animal in all creation that emitted such a vague, indecisive sound.

"Er . . . I'm not sure if you'd remember me or not, but I'm the reporter from the A. *Journal* who paid you a visit once—oh, about three or four years ago now, I suppose."

"Oh yes?"

"I'm no longer with the A. *Journal*—I now work for the B. *News*. Excuse me, but . . ." He bowed politely and offered his card, which bore the title "Reporter, Performing Arts, B. *News*." Professor Rado, keeping one hand in the breast of his kimono and holding a cigarette with the other, cast a cursory glance at the proffered card but made no move to take it. The journalist could not very well withdraw it, so a brief clash of wills ensued. After a bit, however, the professor seemed to feel the awkwardness of the situation and, throwing aside his cigarette, reached out for the card, albeit without much enthusiasm. As he put it into his sleeve pocket, he looked at it briefly for form's sake, and a slight flicker of interest passed over his normally expressionless face—though this the reporter failed to notice.

"Well, it's nice to see you, Professor! . . . Er. . . . Is there someone with you this evening?. . ."

"Uhh. . . . No. . . ."

"I see. Then you're by yourself?"

"Uhh. . . . Unnh. . . ."

"Really?. . . Then you came this far for the exercise?. . ."

"Uhh. . . . Unnh. . . ."

Another rubbery dialogue was underway. The reporter, how-

154

ever, was used to it by now and was quite unflappable.

"But isn't this quite a distance from your house, sir—you are still living in the same place, I take it?"

"Unnh, the same place."

"Is that so? Do you often come to the park, then?"

"Uhh. . . . No. . . ."

"Really? So you came all the way here tonight on purpose, just to see this show?"

This was what he had really been wanting to ask; but it wasn't so easy to squeeze a clear, precise answer out of the professor.

"Why no, I wouldn't say 'on purpose'. . . ."

"It may seem a strange question, but does this sort of entertainment appeal to someone like yourself more than, say, the average play or film would?"

". . . Well . . . I wouldn't say it appeals to me especially, you know, but . . ."

This last "you know, but . . ." phrase contained a certain hint of human warmth, even if only very slight. In the professor's case, it indicated that he was in an exceptionally good mood. The reporter, finding it strange, glanced up at the other's face and saw something stranger still: this man, who never looked directly at the person he was speaking to, was for some reason gazing straight at him now—shyly, to be sure, with a timid, girlish gaze, but still right at him. And on his lips was an amiable smile! It may have been an attempt to mask his embarrassment at having been discovered in a ridiculous situation. At any rate, it was extraordinary. Almost creepy.

Then the next item on the program began, and the two men fell silent and turned toward the stage. The reporter had by now changed seats and was sitting right beside the professor. The entire troupe was performing a musical comedy, employing special magic effects, entitled "Growing Young Again." It was apparently the grand finale of the evening. The journalist was thoroughly bored by this kind of thing, but he pretended to be watching with rapt attention, while actually observing his companion in the next seat. As usual, the professor's expression betrayed no noticeable interest in what he was watching, yet he never looked away and seemed in fact quite intent on the performance. For a man whose permanently gloomy face made one wonder just what pleasure he could find in life to be watching a thing like this so patiently surely implied an element of enjoyment, even if he gave no outward sign of it. If so, then what was it that he found appealing? Scholars, the reporter had discovered, often took pleasure in very simple, childish things, so perhaps the professor simply liked the variety acts themselves. Or was there one particular girl in the troupe to whom he had taken a fancy?

Drawn by curiosity, the reporter kept him company till the very end. The professor, for his part, had watched each boring number on the program with quiet determination right up to the finale. Naturally the two of them left the theater together and began walking in the direction of Hirokoji.

"Er, are you going back by tram, Professor?"

"Uhh. . . . Unnh. . . ."

"Then I'll see you as far as the tram stop. . . ."

Being seen off may well have been bothersome to him, but since, as always, he gave no clear answer, the reporter brashly tagged along. He was racking his brains trying to find some topic to keep the conversation going, when suddenly there came a sound from the professor's mouth: "Uhh . . ."—followed by a sort of rumbling in his throat.

"Yes?" cried the reporter, welcoming this show of enthusiasm on the part of his companion, who seemed to be trying to say something.

"Uhh. . . . By the way. . . ."

"Yes?"

"You report on the performing arts?. . ."

"Yes. . . ."

"Are you always going to places like that?"

"I wouldn't say always, but I have quite a few friends in that troupe, and I happened to be nearby, so I dropped in."

"I see. . . ," said the professor, and after a moment's pause continued: "There's somebody called Ikuno Mayumi—danced in that last number. . . ."

"Oh, really? Which one was he?"

"No, no. It's a woman—tall, with bobbed hair, wearing a costume made out of the American flag. . . ."

"Ohhh, is that so?. . . I'm afraid I don't know her. You say the name is Ikuno Mayumi?"

"Unnh, that's what it says on the program."

Hmm. . . . He'd have to keep an eye on this fellow. The actress he'd mentioned was exceptionally good-looking, from anybody's point of view. The journalist himself had seen her on stage tonight for the first time and was surprised to find such a beautiful girl in the troupe. She was probably twenty-two or -three; her legs under the short skirt were shapely, and her whole body was well proportioned. The only defect one might complain of was that her features were too typically "Greek": there was nothing cute, in the usual sense, about her. She had an air of refinement, but a certain doll-like stiffness went with it.

"Oh? Well, I suppose she must be a pupil of Muyusai's. There are quite a few former members of the old musical revue in that company; but if she were one of them, I should have recognized her."

"Uhh. . . ." Again that rumbling from the professor's throat. "Listen, d'you think you could find out a little about her for me?"

"I beg your pardon?"

"There's something . . . mmmm . . . something a bit odd about her."

"Odd?"

"You didn't notice?"

"What do you mean? I didn't notice anything in particular. . . ."

"She was the only actress who didn't have a single line to say, wasn't she?"

"Really? How observant of you."

"It's always that way."

"Oh? So you've seen her quite a few times, then?"

"Uhh. . . . Unnh. . . ."

"You've taken quite a fancy to her, haven't you?" The words almost slipped from his mouth, but he checked the impulse and instead gave the professor a little more line:

"Maybe she's a deaf-mute."

"And there's another odd thing: she's never showed her bare feet—not even once!"

"Her bare feet?"

"Unnh. . . ."

They had at last reached the tram stop, but the professor showed no signs of wanting to get on; instead, he began to walk in the direction of Ueno, talking to his companion all the while. The words dripped from his lips with appalling slowness, so that it was no easy task to listen patiently until he'd finished and some sort of comprehension was possible. But piecing together the odds and ends of his fragmentary speech, and adding his own conjectures, the reporter came up with roughly the following account.

Muyusai's troupe was constantly on tour, going from the home islands through Korea and Manchuria and then back again. Ever since discovering Ikuno Mayumi two or three years earlier, the professor had gone to see her perform whenever the troupe came to Tokyo. Sometimes he went to see the same program on two or three evenings in succession, and after a while he began to notice something. The roles Mayumi played—for instance, the beautiful woman who is sawed in half, or the Headless Beauty, or the woman in the magic trunk—all required her only to smile, without saying a word. In addition, she sometimes appeared in ballet or musical numbers in which, again, she always played wordless parts only. At first the professor thought that, though lovely to look at, she must be so dim that she couldn't learn the simple lines required. All the same, it was odd that she never said a single word—so perhaps she was deaf-and-dumb? But no, this didn't seem to be the case; for though she never sang solo in the musical revues, she did sometimes join in the chorus. Thinking she might just be mouthing the songs, he took pains to get a seat as near the front as possible and so was able to ascertain with his own ears that she was indeed singing in her natural voice.

There was, however, one single occasion on which Mayumi played a role that obliged her to say some lines, and fairly long ones at that. It was the part of an old beggar woman with a harsh, nasal voice. She came on stage covered with dirt and with a kerchief over her head, and probably the only person in the audience who saw through the disguise was the professor. The rest of the spectators had no idea it was Mayumi, and greeted every line delivered by the beggar woman with peals of laughter. That was how true to life her nasal speech seemed: the role was a great hit. Yet for some reason Mayumi's name did not appear on the program; instead, there was the name of some nonexistent actress. The professor slapped his thigh, pleased at the thought that he had at last found out the secret this beautiful actress was hiding. Ah, so *that* was it! Some disease—syphilis, perhaps—

must have eaten away the inside of her nose.

But there was one more thing he did not understand, namely, why the girl never showed her bare feet. Actually, it was this that had first caught his attention and particularly bothered him, since he was by nature a devout admirer of the female foot. The other girls, when emerging from the magic box or cabinet, were usually bare-legged from the calf down, but Mayumi always wore thin stockings. When five or six girls were doing a dance number together, the others were, again, all barefoot, while she alone wore light silk ballet slippers. Since she could do a toe dance gracefully, there was no question of her being lame. Then one time in a garden-party scene, a great number of actresses appeared on stage in light cotton summer kimonos with bare feet; but even here Mayumi was wearing split-toed *tabi* socks. This prompted the professor to think that it was only an affectation on her part, that she probably just disliked showing her naked feet. Yet he still wasn't entirely convinced, and the solution to the mystery of Mayumi's feet remained in doubt.

"Well, it's an interesting story. I wouldn't mind looking into it a bit myself, if you'd like."

"Uhh. . . . Unnh. . . . I'd appreciate that. . . ."

"Nothing to it. I can find out just by asking a member of the troupe."

"And you won't put it in the newspaper?"

"No, no, of course not. I mean, it'd be cruel to write about that voice of hers, with her being so good-looking."

That evening the professor impressed on the journalist earnestly, variously, and at great length how important it was for him *not* to put anything in the paper, and how anxious he was to hear the results of the investigation in person. He made the same point again when he said goodbye as he boarded the tram at Ueno: "So it'll be all right, then? I'm counting on you!"

Professor Rado and the Beautiful Actress with the Nasal Voice: here was something to arouse anyone's curiosity! It would make an incredible human-interest story for the third page of his paper—what a pity he'd promised not to use it. Partly for the sheer fun of it, then, the reporter began to pursue his investigation, casually making inquiries among his friends in the troupe. It turned out that the professor had been quite right: there *was* something wrong with Mayumi's nose, resulting in that peculiar twangy sound. On the other hand, no one had any positive information about her feet. The reason was that she had never let anyone backstage see her barefoot; apparently she even insisted on taking her bath in absolute privacy. So while there must be something the matter with her feet, no one could say just what. There *had* been one actress who was especially close to her; and this woman was supposed to have said that, on the sole occasion when she managed to take a bath together with Mayumi, she had caught a glimpse of her feet and noticed that one or two toes on either the right or the left foot were missing. Once that story had spread among the company, the general view was that she suffered not only from syphilis but from leprosy as well. Thus, despite her great beauty, she was naturally unwilling to have much to do with other people; and the men in the troupe also kept their distance from her. Or so the story went.

"I don't know whether it's true or not, but everybody just feels uncomfortable around her and stays away," one of the actors told the reporter.

"Well, but what about her skin color? Does it have a purplish sheen to it, in a strong light? I mean, is it sort of shiny?"

"Not at all. She's got a very pale, delicate complexion. Just looking at it, it's really pretty. . . . Some people say that's a bad sign—her skin looks *too* good."

"If it *is* true, I feel awfully sorry for her."

"More than that—it's a real waste! You don't find girls as good-looking as that just anywhere."

One afternoon two or three days later, the reporter paid a visit to Professor Rado at his house in the suburbs and found himself facing him once again across the low table in that well-remembered sitting room.

"Isn't there some doctor she goes to regularly somewhere?" the professor asked after hearing the report on Mayumi. His face was, as usual, dull and expressionless, but he didn't seem particularly shocked by the news.

"Some doctor?"

"Uhh. . . . Unnh. . . . You could find out for sure by asking him. . . ."

"That's a rather tall order, sir. She probably doesn't have her own doctor."

"I wonder about those missing toes. . . . Leprosy leaves a particular kind of sore, you know. . . ."

"That'd be hard to find out, too—they say she doesn't let anybody see her feet. . . ."

"Hmph." The professor looked toward the flower bed outside and continued: "I can find out for myself if I have to. . . . Uhh. . . . In fact, I could do it without moving a step from here, if I only had the proper materials. . . ."

"By proper materials, you mean . . . ?"

"The leprosy bacteria are concentrated most heavily in nasal mucus. If we had a handkerchief or paper tissue she'd blown her nose on, we could tell."

"Really?—I didn't know that. I might be able to get hold of one by asking somebody in the troupe to help—the next time she has a cold or something. . . ."

"Uhh. . . . Would you do that, then? I'd pay whoever it was fifty yen for it. . . ."

About two weeks later, the journalist succeeded in stealing one of Mayumi's handkerchiefs with the aid of a certain actor; the fifty yen was reportedly divided equally between the two of them. But there was never any word from Professor Rado as to the results of the microscopic examination; and after the Mu-yusai troupe split up in June while on tour in the provinces, Mayumi's whereabouts were unknown. Nevertheless, the ever-curious reporter decided to pay the professor a visit one day around the end of August. It seemed highly unlikely that he would know anything about her, but still. . . . At any rate, the would-be caller was turned away at the door, the houseboy inform-ing him that it was "not convenient for the professor" to see him just then. He went two more times and always got the same reply, so he hit on the idea of bribing the parlormaid he had spied upon that time several years before, who was still working in the house. According to her, the professor had recently mar-ried, and his bride was a woman some twenty years younger than himself. The new lady of the house was undeniably pretty; but she also seemed to be very pleased with herself—probably proud of her good looks—and she had always acted very coldly toward the maids. In fact, she had never spoken a word to any of them: when she needed something done, she gave the orders to her husband by means of a nod or a look, and he would then tell the maids what to do. Yet when the two of them were shut up in their room together, the maids could catch faint sounds of them blathering away at each other, through the tightly closed door. The long and short of it was that their new mistress was "right proud of herself."

"Well, of all the dirty . . . ! Using somebody as much as he likes, and then turning him away at his front door! Just who does he think he is?" The reporter was angry, so angry in fact that he decided to climb over the hawthorn hedge at the back and sneak up under the northern window. The bushes were covered with summer leaves, and the glass panel and curtains were half open—just right for peeping through. This gave him quite a good view of what was going on inside.

On top of the chopping-block desk where the parlormaid had once perched, there now sat Mme. Mayumi, pajama-clad, swinging her legs to and fro. Professor Rado, wearing his postal clerk's smock, was underneath, on his knees, fiddling at her naked left foot with both hands. The reporter was just barely able to see what the professor was holding—a toe, made of wax or rubber, and almost indistinguishable from the real thing!

"See? It looks just like one of your own toes. What do you think?. . . Does it fit all right? It doesn't hurt, does it?" The professor spoke in a sweet, coaxing voice as he fitted the object onto Mayumi's foot.

"Whny nho, hinht doesnh't hurnt ha binht."

And now for the first time the reporter heard Mayumi's voice, dripping from those sculpted lips.

ADF-3960